MON

AUG 1 4 2000

LOST YOUTH

Other books by Robert Scott:

Advertising Murder

LOST YOUTH

•

Robert Scott

AVALON BOOKS
NEW YORK

Published by Thomas Bouregy & Co., Inc.
160 Madison Avenue, New York, NY 10016

Library of Congress Cataloging-in-Publication Data

Scott, Robert, 1947–
    Lost youth / Robert Scott.
        p.   cm.
    ISBN 978-0-8034-9908-9 (hardcover : acid-free paper)
    1. Kidnapping—Fiction.   2. Private investigators—Fiction.
I. Title.

    PS3619.C6835L67   2008
    813'.6—dc22   2008005940

PRINTED IN THE UNITED STATES OF AMERICA
ON ACID-FREE PAPER
BY HADDON CRAFTSMEN, BLOOMSBURG, PENNSYLVANIA

To my children, Angela, Deborah, and Ken.
I believe in you.
Nadia and Kana, my Rotary Youth Exchange
daughters, you have helped to keep me young.
This is for you too.
Love you all.

THANKS:

What you hold in your hand is the result of the collaborative efforts of a number of people. All I did was tell the story. The good folks at Avalon Books have taken my words and helped to make your experience enjoyable.

Special thanks go to my editor, Erin Cartwright Niumata, who thought that I might have a story worth sharing and who accompanied me through the ups and downs of publishing a first novel. Erin then shepherded me through some radical editing of this second book, all the while preparing for a 'special edition' of her own.

She will have left Avalon by the time you read this to attend to her new family and to engage in other pursuits. She will be missed.

I am most grateful to you, the reader, who makes all this worthwhile. My joy comes from knowing that you have been entertained by what I love to do.

Chapter One
Out of the Blue

"I have your daughter. Pay the ransom or she dies. No cops. I'm serious."

Eric Howes sat on the edge of his rumpled bed, a look of shock and confusion on his face, as the line went dead.

Just after three in the morning, the phone had rung, and the voice on the other end of the line had delivered the terrifying message. The girl had been kidnapped. There was a ransom of one million dollars. Her life hung in the balance.

The problem for Eric was that he did not have a daughter. He had managed to remain celibate, despite valiant efforts to change the situation. He knew for a certainty that he had no children.

This was obviously a wrong number. Under ordinary circumstances, Eric would have cursed the caller loud and long, whether he was heard or not, and would have gone back to sleep. That was not an option this time. He would not get any sleep until he had discharged his duty. No matter what, he knew in his heart of hearts that to ignore this early-morning call could mean the loss of a young life.

Unfortunately, his caller had been quite clear about the fact that there was to be no police involvement. The only details Eric had were that a kidnapping had taken place, and that a price had to be paid. The caller obviously intended to call back with details of where the ransom was to be left and how the girl was to be retrieved.

"Who is this girl? Where is she from? And who does this pervert think I am? What am I going to do?"

Eric heard himself asking the questions. He felt his heart pounding in his chest as he contemplated the consequences of inaction or a wrong move on his part. He hoped that there would be answers very soon—before it was too late.

Eric picked up the phone and called his friend, Jack. He knew he would have to endure a loud, angry reception after rousing his buddy, but this was more important, and he was confident the friendship could handle the excitement.

The phone on the other end of the line rang and rang. His level of anxiety rose with each jarring reverberation. He was about to hang up after the tenth ring, when a hoarse voice asked over the receiver, "Who are you? What do you want? Make it fast, and make it good."

"Um, hi, Jack. It's Eric. Now before you hit the ceiling, I'm sorry to wake you up, but we've got a real problem."

"What do you mean, 'we'? You've got a problem. I don't have a problem, other than the fact that I've been roused from a sound sleep. I was actually having a half-decent dream that was promising to lead to some interesting romantic involvements, and you have the nerve to call me at . . ."

Eric could hear his friend moving things around on what he could only assume was a bedside table.

"My God, man, you get me up at three thirty to tell me you have a problem. Couldn't this wait for a while, like until normal folks are awake and have had their coffee?"

"Look, Jack, I just got this strange phone call. I don't want to get too dramatic on you so early in the day, but I think it's safe to assume that this is a matter of life and death."

Jack Elton rubbed his eyes as he lay with the phone cradled between the pillow and his right ear. He kicked off the covers, grasped the receiver, and slowly sat up.

Reaching for the lamp, he immediately regretted thinking he needed the extra illumination. He squinted and rested his forehead on his free hand.

"Okay, Eric, let me hear it. And remember, our friendship depends on how urgent you can make this sound. I'll hang up on you the moment this has even the slightest hint of being unimportant."

Eric recounted the details of his recent phone call.

Jack listened, nodding from time to time as if his friend could see him.

"That's the darnedest thing I've ever heard," Jack said. "You figure this guy, whoever he is, misdialed and thought you were this girl's old man?"

"Near as I can figure, that's the story. I can't think of any other explanation."

"You don't think it was some sort of prank? You don't have any friends who might want to pull a really stupid stunt, just to get you all worked up?"

"Only guy I can think of who'd do a thing like that is you, Jack."

"Well, it sure as blazes wasn't me. You know the girl's name?"

"No, that's just the point." Eric's voice betrayed the frustration and deep concern that was rising within him. It almost sounded as if he was accusing Jack of complicating things.

"So what have we got so far? You get a phone call. The life of someone's daughter is in peril. Whoever Daddy is has to raise a million bucks in a hurry, and the guy who's in charge of this little scheme doesn't know that he's barking up the wrong tree, so to speak. Sounds like fun."

"I wish I could share your enthusiasm about it all." Eric was beginning to perspire. He wiped his forehead with the back of his hand.

"Eric, let's do this. Later this morning, you drop by my office. We'll do a little strategizing and assess the resources we have available to us. I figure this guy is smart enough to assume that a million dollars will take a little time to get together, so he's not likely to call back right away. We should have a few hours anyway, before the banks open. Come see me at seven. I'll have the coffee pot on."

"Forget that, Jack. I've tasted the stuff you try to brew. I'll drop by Timmie's and pick up some decent coffee and a few doughnuts. See you in a few hours."

"Yeah. Don't remind me. I gotta get a little more shut-eye."

The line went dead.

Eric did not sleep. He could not sleep. Somewhere, a young woman was being held hostage by a man who thought he had devised a good get-rich-quick scheme. And he wasn't even aware that, already, he had made his first mistake.

Not only had the kidnapper not connected with the person he thought was the source of the cash but, if he was serious about carrying out his threat, he had made it impossible for his intended victim to comply.

Eric paced the floor until almost six. After dressing, he headed out along the old highway toward the city. On the way he picked up two coffees and a half dozen doughnuts for the meeting with Jack.

He pulled to the curb on the outskirts of the city just before seven. The building where Jack lived and worked showed signs of age. White clapboard was chipped in spots. There was evidence that graffiti had been painted over more than once. At ground level, the window of the thrift shop was dark. The store would not open for another two hours.

Eric opened the door that led to the stairs. Jack's office was on the second floor. His apartment was on the third. Fluorescent tubes flickered in the hall leading to the door with the frosted glass window proclaiming JACK ELTON— LEGAL SERVICES.

Until Jack had been called upon to solve the murder of Rhonda Fukushima two years ago, his work had not been well known in the city, and the ex-cop had found himself, when he wasn't acting as a process server, dealing with the problems his friends faced and getting them out of hot water with the law.

Jack had managed to build a small clientele since then, and had made a name for himself in the community. The pay was not great, but his clients were appreciative. Jack often wished he had a little more appreciation in his wallet.

He had turned to investigation full time after he had been called to bail out his friend Brendan Biggs.

Brendan had got himself accused of murder. A dead girl, Rhonda Fukushima, had materialized in his office one morning, and the circumstantial evidence pointed to the advertising executive. Jack had not only got Brendan's name cleared, but was instrumental in leading the police to the real culprit.

It was a sad story.

Eric knocked and turned the knob. He used his butt to open the door and swung around into his friend's office. A somewhat rumpled Jack Elton smiled from behind the desk, which was heaped with file folders, notepads, and what appeared to be a week's worth of old newspapers.

"Come in," the private eye said, grinning, and made a sweeping gesture with his right hand. "Put the coffee and stuff down someplace. How about over there?"

Eric moved to the old steel filing cabinet his friend had indicated and did his best to clear a space on top. It appeared that Jack's filing took place on, rather than in, this piece of equipment.

"I see you still have the same housekeeping service," Eric said.

"Best there is at the price I can afford. One of these days, I'll be able to fire myself and get better help keeping the place clean. . . . Okay, break out the supplies and let's talk about this little puzzle you've brought me."

Eric gave Jack a paper cup of coffee. He tore the tape off the box of doughnuts and held it out in front of his friend.

"Napkin?" Jack offered a box of tissues.

"Don't mind if I do." Eric snatched a couple of the thin paper sheets and pulled up an old wooden chair. He placed his cup and jelly doughnut on the only piece of open real estate on his side of the desk.

The two men ate in silence.

Jack opened the doughnut box after he had finished his first pastry and selected another. "So, let's get down to business. Thanks for the fine breakfast, by the way."

A muffled "welcome" came from sugar-dusted lips as Eric reached for his coffee.

"So, what do you think I can do about this situation that's been forced upon you?"

Eric put down his half-finished doughnut. "I'm thinking we need to find out if someone has actually been abducted. Maybe some of your connections can do a little behind-the-scenes work to see who has gone missing in the past day or two. Once we've got a name, we can go from there. Contact Daddy. Find out why anyone might think he would make a good target. Let him deal with it from there."

A knowing smile came to the investigator's lips.

"Yeah, sure. We help the perpetrator get in touch with the mark, and then we just walk away? You don't sound, or look, like you are going to be able to detach yourself from this thing until it's resolved. For my part, I'm not about to start what I don't intend to finish. Besides, it sounds like this case is going to require a go-between. From what we know so far, your kidnapper is convinced that you are the girl's father, and he won't take your word for it that he's got a wrong number. You are in this thing for the duration, and I guess I'm taking you up on the invitation to come along on the ride."

"I appreciate it. I really do," Eric said. "And you're right. If this isn't some sort of twisted joke, I want to see the girl safe and this guy caught. What do we do now?"

Jack thought for a moment. He reached for the doughnut box again and fingered the two remaining pastries before removing the chocolate walnut crunch. "Let me talk to Valerie. I'll ask if she can nose around in the police computers to see if anything shows up."

Valerie Cummins was the love of Jack's life. They had solidified their relationship when he was dealing with the murder in the office tower. Jack wasn't anxious to abuse the relationship, but the present situation seemed desperate enough to make asking a favor reasonable. He knew Valerie's abilities were more than equal to the task.

The up side would be that Jack would get to talk to his female friend and, perhaps, get her involved enough so that they could be together a little more.

"You'll make her understand that the police can't be involved, won't you?" There was panic in Eric's voice.

"Don't worry. I know Valerie well enough to know that she can keep a secret. Besides, there isn't a case if there isn't a victim. We don't even know if this is real or not. You head back home, and wait for a phone call. If it isn't me, it might be your early morning threatener. I want you to be careful to get every detail of anything he might say. You hear anything before I get back to you, give me a call. Take my card. It has my cell number on it."

Jack had learned his lesson dealing with the Fukushima case without the aid of wireless communication. It had been a regular frustration during the investigation to have to track down a pay phone. Lately phone booths were becoming scarcer. Jack's cell phone had become a constant, and comforting, companion.

Eric stuffed the business card in his shirt pocket and drained the rest of his coffee. Jack took the cup and tossed it into an already overflowing wastebasket. He grabbed a ruler from his desk and used it to ram the garbage deeper.

"Gotta clean up around here . . . one of these days," he muttered to himself as his visitor rose to leave.

"Let me know what you find out from Valerie," Eric said over his shoulder as he turned toward the door.

"Can I have the last doughnut?" Jack asked.

"Sure. Knock yourself out. I'll be waiting by the phone."

"Sounds like a plan."

Eric let himself out. He slouched down the stairs and crawled into his car. The lack of sleep from the night before was starting to catch up with him. The fact that he worked from home would be a comfort throughout the rest of a day that had begun far too early.

Chapter Two
On the Road Again

It wasn't long before Jack knew what his next step would be. His call to Valerie went unanswered. He hung up the phone and headed for the door.

An unanswered phone after eight in the morning meant that the young police officer, with blond hair in a ponytail that Jack loved to touch, was working somewhere in the city. He would have to track her down. He drove to the police department.

He had been fortunate to be able to get a replacement for the old "beater" that had sufficed for many years. It had served him well but, when Valerie came into his life, it seemed to Jack that he needed something a little newer and safer. He was encouraged in this by Val, who would constantly point out all the infractions he was committing with his vehicle.

At the police station, Jack parked and walked in through

the main entrance. He was known to most of the members of the force, either because of his relationship with Valerie or his past history as a cop, blemished though it was.

"Hi, Hilda. What's new this morning?"

"Nothing I can tell you about, cowboy." The officer was well past her prime and not in any physical shape to be chasing felons. She had been hired only recently to handle the string of inquiries that came to the department from the public and the media.

It was Hilda's job to run interference for the real cops and only let through those who had a valid reason to speak with the folks behind the locked door that she controlled with a button under her desk.

"I'm not looking for any leads today, Hilda. There is a certain officer I need to talk to, though."

"Cotton and Venables."

"What's that?"

"You're looking for Cummins. She's on traffic duty at the corner of Cotton and Venables, or at least she's supposed to be. If she's on the move, you'll find her patrolling on Venables somewhere. We've had a lot of speeders there lately, particularly in the school zone. Good luck."

"Thanks, Hilda. You're a peach."

"Don't press your luck. And keep within the speed limit. Cummins is supposed to ticket you, even if you are her sweetie, if you exceed the limit."

"I'll bear that in mind. Thanks for the driving tip."

Jack blew Hilda a kiss and leaned on the heavy glass door that led to the outside. The receptionist watched after him and gave a deep sigh before returning to her paperwork.

The traffic was starting to thin after the initial morning rush. Arteries into town began to fill just after six each morning, and movement was slow until after nine. Jack was thankful that the city was enjoying one of its few rain-free fall days.

The corner that Hilda had indicated was empty of police vehicles when Jack arrived. While traffic was slow in the area, it was never so slow that those with places to go could not exceed the posted limit by another ten miles per hour.

Jack turned the corner onto Venables and headed to the school zone. As he approached a playground, the familiar shape of a white Crown Victoria, with POLICE written across the trunk, alerted him to the location of his quarry.

The light bar was ablaze and Jack could see the slender blond officer leaning over to address a frustrated driver who had been caught in her web.

Probably best to wait this out, Jack thought to himself as he slackened his speed and pulled up behind the cruiser.

He turned off his motor and watched Valerie walk back to her car and slide into the front seat. Jack knew what came next.

Valerie picked up her radio mike and read from the papers she had taken from the speeder. She would want to know if there were outstanding warrants and if this driver was a habitual traffic offender. If the name on the license didn't match that on the registration, did this guy have a right to be driving the car? The registration would be checked before any citations were issued.

Valerie continued to sit and write. Jack knew that the information she was waiting for had been retrieved when he saw her grab the mike again and speak into it briefly.

Some more writing and she was back out of the cruiser and walking with purpose toward the car she had pulled over. She had her clipboard out and was tearing off a familiar-looking top sheet, which she handed through the car window.

Jack imagined her level tone of voice as she politely explained how the offender could deal with the ticket, and what his options were, if he decided to fight it. She would conclude with a polite "Have a good day" before returning to her cruiser and reporting that she was "clear."

At least he was stopped by a cute officer, Jack thought to himself. *That should count for something toward a good day, no matter how lousy the guy might feel for being caught.*

As Valerie approached the side of her car, Jack flashed his lights. Until now, she had given no indication of having seen him waiting.

She looked up, smiled, and walked to the window of his car.

"Good morning, sir." She smiled. "Coming to turn yourself in, are you?"

"I surrender to you, Officer Cummins. Do with me what you will."

"Okay, mister, to what do I owe this early morning visit?"

"Can you give me a minute of your time before you call in clear?"

She looked at her watch.

"Alright, but we'd better use my car. It looks better that way."

"I'll follow you anywhere," Jack replied with a grin.

In the patrol car, Jack explained Eric's early-morning call and the puzzle that they were facing.

"Can you check around and let me know if there are any missing persons that might fit our limited description? We're looking for a female. She's young enough that her parents would still be alive. Could be a baby. Could be a child. Might be a woman in her teens or older. That's how helpful our caller has been. We're probably looking for someone who hasn't been gone long. Maybe one or two days."

"I can tell you right now that at this morning's briefing there was no mention of anyone we should be on the lookout for. She could be from a whole different city or even another country. Where did the call originate?"

"Can't tell. Eric said nothing showed up on his caller ID. All he got from the phone company was one of those taped messages saying that the calling party could not be identified."

"I'll keep my eyes open. But don't be holding your breath. You may end up very short of air before I have anything. There is a good chance that if there is a missing person, no one has noticed that she's missing yet."

"I'll wait for your call."

"Hey, I didn't say you should be like that. You can call

me any time you want. We may just have to talk about something other than business."

"I can live with that. Now you'd better get back to protecting the fine citizens of our fair city."

"Call me, Jack. Tonight."

"Yes sir, Officer Cummins, sir." Jack gave an awkward salute and slipped out of the police cruiser.

Back in his own car again, Jack watched as Valerie called in her status and turned off the light bar. He watched her pull away from the curb and then restarted his engine. If there was a missing woman, and she was anything even close to resembling Valerie, he knew that someone would be desperate to get her back. He wondered if he would be able to help them before it was too late.

He pulled away from the curb and headed down the next block. He would call Eric to fill him in on what he had done so far and find out if the mystery caller had been in touch again.

Jack drove toward the nearest coffee shop. He could use his cell phone in the parking lot.

The familiar red scroll lettering of the popular coffee shop chain that was named after an old-time hockey player came into view, and Jack signaled to turn in.

The drive-through was crowded. Jack took his place in the line of cars and dialed Eric.

The phone rang three times before Eric's groggy voice came on the line. "Nothing so far, Jack. You got anything?"

"I've got people working on it."

"You mean Val is working on it."

"There you go. She says there were no reports of missing people in the last eighteen hours or so. She would have heard at the morning briefing if there were."

"Maybe it's just a lame joke after all," Eric said, sounding hopeful.

"Let's hope so. I'm all for a little excitement, but never at the expense of some innocent soul."

"If it weren't for the innocent ones, there'd be no crimes to solve, Jack."

"I guess you've got a point there. I'm going to pick up a coffee and head back to my office. Let me know if you hear anything. Right now, the trail, if there ever was one, is cold as ice. Gotta go. I'm up to the menu board. Gotta place my order and move on."

"I'll let you know if anything develops, Jack."

Jack placed an order for an extra large coffee, "double-double," and moved to the pickup window. His mind raced as he contemplated the possible scenarios that might present themselves.

"No use conjuring up some fantastic scene until I have something to back up the story. Still, there are plenty of crackpots out there. Never hurts to try and be prepared."

He took the cup that was offered and handed his money to the girl wearing the headset. She handed back some change and smiled at him briefly. Then she seemed to lose interest and turned to prepare another order.

Jack pocketed his money and drove back out onto the street. He rounded the next corner and headed west again, back to his office.

His building was soon in sight. He looked for an open spot in traffic so he could pull his now-famous U-turn, which would bring him alongside the curb in front of the thrift shop.

Before he got that opportunity, his cell phone rang. He snapped it open with his free hand.

"Jack here."

"Jack, it's Eric. He called." The voice was high and shaky.

Chapter Three
No Victim, No Crime

"Hang on. I'm about ten minutes away from your place. I'm coming over."

"Okay. Use the guest parking around the back. You know where it is?"

"Gotcha. Yeah, I've been there before. Remember?"

"I'll be waiting."

Jack found a spot in the parking lot behind Eric's apartment. He walked toward the building and tossed his empty coffee cup in a Dumpster by the back door.

The place was well secured. Visitors could only enter by the front door. There were no names by the intercom and, unless you knew the apartment number of the person you wanted, you were out of luck. Jack punched the number of Eric's apartment and, after a brief exchange with his friend, heard the buzzing of the door lock.

He went in and took the stairs to the third floor.

Eric was standing in the hallway when Jack stepped

out of the stairwell. He greeted his friend with a voice that conveyed urgency, and the two went into the little apartment.

Jack sat at one end of the white couch with his back to a window. Eric took an easy chair across from his friend. He offered coffee, but Jack was still feeling the buzz of all the caffeine he had had so far.

"So, what have you got for me?" Jack asked.

"Like I told you, the guy called back about twenty minutes ago."

"And . . ."

"Same as before. 'I got your girl. She's okay for the time being. I want a million or she dies.' I tried to tell him that he had the wrong number, but he said he didn't believe me. Accused me of trying to pull a fast one. Said he'd give me some time to get the money together. Asked if I'd spoken to the cops. I told him I hadn't."

Eric's face was solemn. His hair had been mussed by too much running of his hands through it. He shifted uneasily, crossing and uncrossing his legs.

"Did he say anything that might help us to determine whether he's on the up-and-up? Strike that. He's obviously not. What I mean is, can we be sure he actually has someone?"

"I've got a name, I think. For the girl, I mean. He let it slip that her name was Jan or Jen. I'm not sure which. He has a slight accent. I'm not good at those sorts of things, so I can't place it."

"Well, that's a start, at least. He didn't, by any chance, let a last name slip?"

"No. I'm sure of that. He did sound like he knew

whoever he thought I was pretty well. He spoke as if he had at least met the girl's father at some point."

"Who is this guy? What's his game?" Jack asked. "He seems in no particular rush to get his money, yet he's threatening murder if the dad doesn't pay. I think he's bluffing."

"What do you mean?" Eric sat forward, his eyes focused on Jack.

"I think it's this way. The guy has an interest in upsetting Daddy. Either that or he's got a thing for the girl and enjoys having her around. He's not in this for the money. He's doing this to get back at someone."

Jack tapped his forehead with an index finger. His brow was seriously creased. The fingers of the other hand drummed the arm of the sofa.

"He doesn't want the money?" Eric asked.

"I'm not saying that," Jack replied. "He'll take it, if he can get it, and be very happy. What I'm saying is that it's an add-on. The abduction's the thing. He wants to scare someone. And when he's done, he'll have the means to go away somewhere and live out his life in luxury. Of course, if he's in any way unstable, the girl's life is still in danger. We have to go on that assumption. Let's not underestimate this guy or do anything that might send him over the edge."

"He can do that?" Eric asked.

"Not if I can help it. He only thinks he can do it. He's going to get caught, I think. If we can figure out who he is, and who he's got, not necessarily in that order."

Eric seemed to relax a little, but the unanswered questions still hung in the air over their discussion.

"Why would he call you? Why would he think you are the girl's father? If he misdialed once, surely he would get it right the second time, unless he has bad information," Jack said.

"Maybe he's just using Redial," Eric suggested.

"That might work as long as he never calls anyone else from that phone. I can't imagine that happening. No, he's got it written down somewhere. In a little black book, on a Rolodex, or in an old phone book."

"I'm the only one who has ever had this number," Eric said. "The exchange didn't exist before this complex was built." Eric shifted in his chair.

"Then it's a mistake on paper or in this guy's head, and right now we don't know which. We'll have to wait on our source at the police department." A faint smile crossed Jack's lips.

"You sure have a strange way of referring to your girl when you're on business. You think I've forgotten you already told me Valerie was on the case. And you always smile when you think about her. You never smile when you think about Detective Sergeant What's-his-face."

"Okay, ya got me," Jack said. "But there isn't a whole lot we can do right now. We have to wait, unfortunately. I wonder if the girl's father has noticed she's missing. Is he in a position to even know she's gone?"

"How do you mean?" It was Eric's turn to demonstrate the brow-pleating maneuver.

"Jan, or whatever her name is, is away from home. She isn't in the habit of calling every day. Maybe she only calls on the weekends. She misses one week, and her parents figure she's off with her friends somewhere. It could take a couple of weeks before anyone twigs to the fact that she's gone missing."

"I see what you mean," Eric said.

"This guy who's calling you figures he's giving the father this information. As long as this goes on, and he doesn't figure out that the number is wrong, the parents might not know for days or weeks. If he gets mad enough to try something stupid, he will mess things up for everyone."

"I'm sorry," Eric said. "I wish I'd paid more attention. Maybe there was something I could have picked up on that would help."

"Don't beat yourself up over this. Now that we know what the questions are, we can be listening a little closer for the answers when he calls again. I'm confident he will call again. The weekend's coming. That might help."

"Huh?" Eric looked confused.

"If the parents are expecting a call and it doesn't come, this might be the thing that stirs up their concern. They check around. Find she's gone. Call the cops."

"Um, maybe."

The two men fell silent. Drooping eyelids and nodding heads revealed the fatigue brought on by stress and lack of sleep. A clock on the wall ticked off the passing minutes.

Jack was jarred back to consciousness by a gentle shaking of his shoulder. Eric smiled as his friend roused himself.

"You've been asleep."

"I sort of gathered that. Anything new?" he asked.

"No one has called, if that's what you mean. I dropped off for a while too. I'm feeling rested but no less frustrated."

"Join the club." Jack rubbed his eyes vigorously. "I was heading back to my place when you called me over here. I think I'll give it another try. Maybe Val will call with some sort of a lead."

Jack took the elevator down to the lobby for his exit. Frustration continued to sap his energy.

We need a break, and soon, he thought, as he held the elevator door open for an elderly couple who had just entered the lobby from outside.

Once inside his car, he cranked the engine and headed out to the highway for his trip home. It was past three, and the traffic from town was beginning to become heavier. Heading toward the city, as he was, the cars were moving more quickly and there were noticeably fewer of them.

Before long, Jack was back in front of the old building he called home and office. He locked up the car before heading upstairs.

On the second floor he unlocked the office and stood inside, scanning the interior, as if lost. The answering machine showed no indication of having any messages for its master. He pushed the Play button just in case. The machine had not been lying.

He slumped in his old chair. He held his head in his hands and moved it back and forth as he contemplated the situation that had intruded on his day. Would this thing ever begin to resolve itself? He was beginning to doubt it.

Jack pushed papers around on his desk for a while. He called some folks who he had promised to contact about possible contracts. He had enthusiasm for none of them. He wondered whether he was doing himself a disservice by getting involved with this present mystery. After some thought, he was sure he was doing the right thing. He just wished that the facts would bear out his conviction.

Shortly after five, he decided to go up to his apartment. He left everything where it was—not unusual for Jack. He always left things just as they were. When he came in the next time, they would likely be where he left them. Of course, he might not remember where that was.

Back in his living room, he saw that the answering machine by the phone was flashing its light. A break? Maybe.

He pressed Play.

"Jack, Val here. Call me."

His heart skipped a couple of beats. Was it her voice or was it the possibility that she had some information for him that gave him palpitations? Maybe both.

He punched in her number. It rang once, then—

"Hi, Jack." She sounded upbeat.

"Ah, the wonders of caller ID. What's cookin'?"

"Supper, if you want it. I've got this fierce Mexican chicken thing going and there's more than I can eat in a week."

"No news?"

"Yes, it is nice of me to offer. You're very welcome. And no, I have nothing to report. Are you coming over or not?"

"Sorry about the attitude, but this thing has been playing with my mind all day and I'm not much closer to a solution," Jack said. "Thanks for the invite. I'd love to come over. Can you give me some time to clean myself up? I'm much easier to dine with when I don't smell."

"Sure. How's six thirty?" The cheer was back in her voice again.

"Good for me. See you soon. Don't open your door to strangers."

"Only you," she giggled.

After a shower, a shave, and some clean clothes, Jack was back in the car again. He reflected on how fortunate it was that he'd traded the old one. It couldn't have handled all this excitement.

Soon he was at Valerie's apartment complex. He found a place to park on the street and moments later was standing outside her apartment door, having negotiated all the hurdles necessary to gain admittance to the building.

Valerie opened her door, and the smell of spicy cooking filled the air. They embraced in the hallway, then she ushered him into her apartment.

The table was set. A bottle of white wine stood on the side board, along with two long-stemmed glasses.

"Will you pour?" she asked, seeing that he had noticed the bottle.

"My pleasure, ma'am." He bowed deeply and made a wide arc with one arm.

"Silly."

"You call me that a lot."

"Only 'cause I love you and know you can take it," she said.

"I'll consider that a vote of confidence. Silly me." He batted his eyes and held his hand up to his mouth.

"Silly," she said.

He reached for the corkscrew and began working on the bottle.

Valerie lit candles she had placed on the table and then returned to the small kitchen to deal with the chicken that was giving off the most wonderful aroma.

She placed the casserole on the countertop, then began spooning hot vegetables onto the dinner plates.

"You want to come over here and tell me how much of this you want?" she asked.

Jack walked over to the counter and wrapped his arms around her neck. He stared into her eyes.

"I'll have all of it, please."

"Not me. This," she said, indicating the chicken pieces.

"Aw, I'm disappointed now." He kissed her neck. She squirmed and giggled.

"That tickles," she said and tried to look disapprovingly at him. She failed.

"I believe I'll have just one piece for now, missy." He tried his best to sound like Foghorn Leghorn from the Warner Brothers cartoons.

Valerie prepared his plate and carried it to the table along with her own.

Jack poured the wine.

As they ate, they chatted as people in love will do. The subject of the missing girl did not come up. Jack was glad for the break from problem solving. He was gladder still to be in the presence of this young woman who had so captured his heart in such a short time.

They had been introduced at a party. After working on the murder investigation two years ago, they had encountered one another again at the police station. He was asking questions. She was giving answers.

After that, Jack had taken every opportunity to be where she was, and to look as if he deserved to be there.

He invited her out one afternoon and was surprised when she said yes. The rest was a sort of warm blur that led to this moment, as they looked into each other's eyes by candlelight.

The meal and the wine were soon consumed. Jack helped Valerie clear the dishes. He would have preferred not to get into any discussion of the day's events but knew he would kick himself afterward if he didn't take advantage of this young woman's expertise in the field of crime investigation.

The coffee was poured. The couple retired to the couch. They sat in silence, relaxed in each other's company.

"I'm not sure what to think about this abduction that may, or may not, have taken place," he said after a while.

"Well, that just about kills the mood," she said, not really upset by his comments.

"Sorry, but this thing is going to bother me for some time, and I need your reflections on it."

"Like I told you on the phone, there is nothing in the database and nothing on the assignment board that even closely resembles the situation you described. You know as well as I do that, without a victim, there is no crime. If someone shows up, or rather, fails to show up, we can assume there is a victim and follow that lead. Not much else can be done until then."

"I wish I could bring the police in on this, if anything develops," he said.

"Think a moment. Who can't bring in the department?"

"Well, I can't. Eric can't. The guy said . . ."

"And who does the guy think he's talking to?" She looked him straight in the eye. She was all business now.

"Well, he thinks Eric is Daddy," Jack said.

"Right. If this thing pans out, this is what you have to do . . ."

Valerie laid out a plan that had escaped Jack's thinking processes so far. She warned him to be absolutely sure that some of her assumptions were correct before he considered getting the police involved.

"If I'm right," she added, "he'll never suspect. You gotta find the father too. This may take time. And I hate you."

"What?"

"Look what you've done. You've got me all excited about this thing and, for now, I can't do anything about it."

Jack drove home later that night, content but still questioning whether he should pursue Eric's case or move on to other things. He decided to let the matter rest until the morning.

This proved to be easier said than done.

Once he got back to his apartment and got into bed, he lay awake pondering all the possible permutations of the puzzle. He reflected on the conversations he had had in the past twenty-four hours. He thought about the girl. He thought about Eric and his concern. He thought about Valerie's theory and her wise suggestions about how the police could be involved without the abductor knowing. Mostly he thought about Valerie.

He drifted off into a deep sleep. He didn't notice the flashing light on the answering machine.

Chapter Four
Friday—A Day Early

The weekend was a day away. The weather had been uncertain all week, but at least it had not rained.

Jack was up early. He started the coffee and peered out the window. The uncertain weather was making up its mind. It was definitely going to be wet. The radio said it would remain that way all weekend. People would be able to make hay while the sun shone, starting on Monday.

Jack pulled the curtains closed and headed for the coffee maker. It was then that he noticed the flashing message light on the answering machine. He pressed the button.

"Jack, he called again." Eric's voice hinted at satisfaction but he had been unable to disguise the quaver of anxiety and the hoarseness of fatigue.

Jack poured a coffee and grabbed the portable phone. He sat at the table in what passed for a kitchen, just behind the sofa in the living room. He dialed.

"Eric, it's Jack. Look, I'm sorry I didn't get back to you last night. I was, um, tied up last night and didn't notice your message till just now."

"Checking out your sources will do that, Jack."

"I'm glad you are so understanding." He grabbed a corner of the frayed dressing gown he had thrown on over his naked body and tried to pull it across his chest for a little more warmth.

"Our guy called again," Eric said. "He said he knew I didn't believe he had my daughter. He said I'd know he was telling the truth when she didn't call on the weekend. I pretended to be who he thinks I am and said I needed more time to get the money together."

"What did he say to that?"

"He got kind of tough sounding and said I'd better get a move on. He said I had till Monday and then he was going to tell me where to leave the cash. He didn't say what he might do if I didn't comply. He did say to keep the police out of it."

Jack shifted in the chair. The dressing gown was a little too short, and the seat was vinyl. He had to be careful that he didn't shock his system with a sudden change of temperature from a poorly relocated buttock.

"I think we can work our way around that if only we can get to the point of finding out who the girl is, and who her father is."

"Sounds iffy. How do you propose we work around that, assuming we can figure out who Jan or Jen—or whatever her name is—is?" Eric asked.

Jack reviewed the thoughts Valerie had shared with him

the night before. He tried to sound convincing, though he wasn't entirely sure that they could pull it off.

"So it's important to find the father, and get him to agree to trust us, and to play along."

"Exactly. But we need a break in this case, and we just don't have one yet. I'm not dressed yet. Give me some time. I'll call you later and pick you up. Let's visit the university."

"Do you really think higher education is going to benefit us at this late stage in our lives?" Jack pictured a smile behind Eric's voice. He laughed.

"Probably not, but the registrar is the best one to answer that question."

A while later, Jack and Eric were speeding toward the university. Traffic was moving smoothly and people were more polite, it seemed. Jack wondered if it had anything to do with the fact that the weekend was coming.

"We'll see whether the theory about the girl being away from home has any merit. If she's a student in town, this is probably the first place we should look."

"We might be totally off base about this whole thing. What if we are talking about some little kid?" Eric sounded concerned.

"But remember what he said. There was something about knowing he had the girl because she didn't call. That's important. It confirms that she is away from her parents."

"Or maybe just her dad," Eric added.

They drove onto the campus and found their way to the administration building. A road encircled the center of the site, and they parked in a small lot across from the main doors. Jack was careful to make sure he purchased enough time on the meter.

Inside, the two men introduced themselves, and Jack gave a general overview of what they were trying to discover. A receptionist gave them directions to the registration office.

After speaking to another secretary, a representative of the registrar invited them into her office. They took chairs across from a large mahogany desk. Writing implements and files were neatly arranged. A large computer monitor sat in one corner.

"You need to understand our position, gentlemen. While I am sympathetic to your cause, we are not in the practice of letting just anyone look at our files. In this day and age, we are required by law to protect the privacy of everyone who entrusts their private information to us."

Jack leaned forward to address the woman who, it appeared, was about to deny them any information that might help them in their search for clues.

"Ma'am, it is not my intention to pry into your files and carry away vital information. Let me ask, can you access student names from your computer?"

"Of course." She sounded offended by the suggestion that she was not privy to the details of the student population.

"Can you give me some general information?" he asked.

"Depends on what you need, I guess."

"Can you tell me how many students with the first name Jan or Janice you might have?"

"I can, but you may not be satisfied with the answer."

"Let's see."

The woman tapped away on a keyboard that she pulled

out from under the desk top. She scanned the screen and pressed a few more keys.

"There are one hundred eighty-six Jan or Janice entries."

"Can you try Jen or Jennifer?"

Again the tapping and scanning. Then the disappointing news.

"About two hundred. That includes part-time students and night classes."

"Any girls with those names reported missing?" Eric asked. Wrinkles furrowed his brow.

"None that I know of. Security might be able to help you better, but I doubt it. They usually check with us first, if someone reports a student absent for an extended period of time."

Eric's face fell. Not that a missing person would have made him happy, but he had hoped that they would have a lead of some sort at this point.

Jack thanked the administrator, and both men left the office.

Back on the street, Eric turned to Jack. "I know this may sound silly, but I almost feel sort of guilty that I'm the one with the number that our guy called. I guess I wish it was someone else he called by mistake."

"Don't let it get to you. Think of it this way; maybe some other guy would have dismissed the whole thing and told the guy to do whatever he wanted, and just to leave him alone."

"Well, I wish I could do more."

"You'll probably get the opportunity. Hang in there," Jack said.

He thought it wise to check with security before they

left the campus. Though there was little hope that the news would be any different, they had to cover as many bases as possible before giving up.

The uniformed mountain of a man who greeted them gave no more encouragement than the lady with the desk in the admin building. The only excitement they had had lately was a drunken fight in one of the parking lots the previous Sunday night. There were no reports of missing young women.

"What if he kills her?" Eric asked as they drove back toward the outskirts of the city.

"He's not going to do that. He's waiting for you, I mean her father, to cough up the money. He knows the dad well enough to believe that he can, and will, get the money to save his princess."

"'Course, the problem there is that Dad doesn't know his girl is in trouble and, even if you and I put our savings accounts together, we couldn't come up with even a few thousand bucks."

"You're wrong there."

"How do you mean?" Eric looked at his friend.

"I doubt that we could scratch together more than a few hundred bucks between us."

The gray day grew darker within the confines of Jack's car.

Rain pelted the windshield as they drove along the slickened streets. Pedestrians hunched over and drew coats over their heads or opened umbrellas. Others huddled in doorways or took refuge in stores and offices as the annual rainy season continued to assault the city.

The two men could feel their spirits dive as they

contemplated the possibility of being late for the rescue that they had so hoped would be easier.

"We can always hope the whole thing is a joke," Eric said with no trace of conviction in his voice.

"It's beyond that now, I think." Jack turned up the defroster fan and cranked the heat wide open as he surveyed the road ahead. "A joke would be over by now. This guy keeps calling and dropping hints about what he'll do if the cash doesn't materialize. I think we're dealing with serious stuff, if you ask me. Want some coffee?"

"Why not?" Eric replied. "I've got nothing else to do but sit around and buzz while I wait for something more exciting to happen."

The ringing of Jack's cell phone interrupted their less-than-exciting conversation.

"Grab that, will ya?" Jack said. "It's in the console, there." He indicated the source of the ringing with his right hand.

Eric retrieved the phone and snapped it open.

"Hello?" He listened. "Well, I'm sure that you are a very nice young lady and that sounds exciting, but I think Jack would be a little bit upset if I messed around with his lady friend. Besides, you might handcuff me or something."

He placed the phone in Jack's outstretched hand. "I think it might be a personal call for you."

"Hi, Val. Forgive my friend. He and I are living life on the edge. I mean the edge of boredom. What's up?"

Jack listened. "We're on our way. And, uh, when we're finished, maybe you'll let me know what you said to Eric." A pause, then "Yeah. I'll let him know you didn't mean him. He'll be disappointed."

Jack snapped the phone shut and tossed it in Eric's lap.

"Looks like we may have something to pep up our weekend. The coffee won't be nearly as good at the cop shop, but Val seems to think we might have Dad."

"To the batcave, Robin." Eric drew his head back to simulate a sudden increase in speed and smiled. Things were looking up from the perspective of forward progress, at least.

Valerie was standing on the median at the parking lot entrance as Jack and Eric pulled in. Jack rolled down the window.

"Boy, you must have really messed up. Bumped down to parking lot attendant?" he said.

She ignored him.

"I'm thinking it might be wiser not to be chatting in the station until we need to bring in some of the others. I'm on a break. Let's find a place to get some food. I'm starving," she said, smiling.

"Well, there's a branch office a couple of streets over. They sell soup and sandwiches as well as coffee and doughnuts. Let's go there."

"We don't spend all our time in Timmie's, you know. I hope you'll come to appreciate that once you hear what I have to say."

"Sounds good to me. I can't wait. So is it Timmie's?" Jack asked.

Valerie made a show of being offended but couldn't suppress the smile that had had the power to melt Jack's heart from the very first.

"Race ya," Jack said.

"Arrest ya, if you do," she called back over her shoulder as she headed for her cruiser.

"Such a serious girl," Jack said to Eric with a broad smile.

Jack ordered coffee for himself and the others. Valerie wanted a bowl of soup and a sandwich. Eric settled for a bread bowl filled with stew. Jack offered to pay for it all, and a chicken sandwich for himself.

They selected a table in one corner of the brightly lit restaurant. The interiors of every one of these ubiquitous coffee shops were all the same—metal tables and chairs in green with beige tops. Pictures on the wall featured scenes from the summer camps the franchise sponsored. Posters advertising the latest special or package deal were interspersed with the other wall decorations. A glass case held samples of the non-food wares that could be purchased at the counter: mugs, hats, gift certificates, commemorative coffee cans.

Jack passed out the food.

It was not going to be as private as they might have hoped, but there was a constant din of conversation that would probably mask anything they might say to one another.

"So, what have you got for us?" Jack asked and took a massive bite out of his sandwich.

"At the briefing this morning, something came up that I thought might have something to do with what you've been working on. There's this guy, Herties. He's got a lot of cash, I gather. Made his millions in real estate. Sort of like The Donald, but at the Canadian exchange rate.

"Anyway, he has an in with the chief. Personal friend, I think. He's asking if we can snoop around on the hush-hush. Seems his daughter hasn't called Daddy for cash lately, and he thinks that's a little strange."

"How long's it been since they communicated?" Jack took another mouthful of sandwich and raised his eyebrows to Valerie in a "go ahead" gesture.

"It's been a couple of weeks. She was away with some friends on some sort of sports outing so Mr. Herties didn't think anything of it the first week. But after something like that, his daughter is pretty much tapped out financially and needs a refill. She doesn't work, part-time or otherwise."

"Sounds like she's a little spoiled," Eric offered.

"Not sure about that," Valerie said. "I get the impression that the father wants her to get a good education. Figures work might interfere with her studies."

"But going away with her friends doesn't?" Jack asked.

"You'd have to talk to Mr. Herties about that, but I think he and the girl's mother have made it clear that she can only have a social life on the weekends."

"Where do we find this guy?" Jack asked, wiping mayonnaise from his hands.

"That's easy. His office is in the penthouse of the Herties Tower, downtown. You can't miss it. It's the one with the gold-colored windows that cause all the pile-ups on the highway when the sun's just right. The windows reflect the sun, and blind drivers going west in the morning and east in the afternoon." Valerie had obviously had to deal with some of those motor vehicle accidents.

"Would he be there this afternoon?" Eric asked.

"Should be. He gave us his private office number, in case we got anything."

"Will we still be able to work our plan to involve you guys officially?" Jack wasn't particularly anxious to do this on his own. He was noted for trying to keep the police informed and involved. When it came to the law and arrests, his experience helped him only in knowing what might come next. Since his unceremonious dismissal from the force, he liked to keep folks happy. His reputation had been damaged badly enough.

"Right now we're only supposed to keep our ears to the ground. There is nothing going on that might upset the guy who has Jennifer," Val said.

"That's her name?" Jack asked.

"Yeah, Jennifer Herties," Val said.

"Well, buddy," Jack looked at Eric, who had just finished the last morsel of his bread bowl and was wiping his hands with a wad of paper napkins from the dispenser. "I guess we've got our orders. Let's go and see Mr. Herties. I hope he'll trust us with his daughter's life."

"I hope he doesn't have a heart attack when he hears why his daughter hasn't been calling," Eric offered.

Jack stood and bowed dramatically.

"Thank you so much, Officer Cummins. You have done a fine job. We'll let you know what we discover. Depending on Herties, we'll have to see what happens next."

"Be careful, guys," Val said, adding, "and be polite, Jack. He's got a lot on his plate right now."

"In his pockets too," Jack answered. He turned on his heel.

Eric followed.

Valerie was left to clean up the table.

"Thanks, guys," she muttered. "This is just what I went to the police academy to learn how to do."

The rain had let up by the time Jack and Eric got to the parking lot of the doughnut shop. Jack opened the door of the car for Eric and headed around to the driver's side.

"Aw, nuts."

"What is it?" Eric asked from inside the car.

"Gotta get something. I'll be right back." Jack sprinted toward the restaurant. He met Valerie as she was coming out the door. They talked briefly. She checked her notepad. Jack wrote something on an envelope he produced from his jacket pocket. They smiled. Jack walked back to the car and got in.

"Got the special number. It might come in handy."

"Herties' private phone?"

"That's the one."

Chapter Five
Know Victim, Know Crime

Traffic in the city on a Friday afternoon can be a real challenge. Tradition has it in Vancouver that offices close a little earlier, or right on time, and everyone exits for the weekend.

This Friday was no different from the others. Jack and Eric spent most of their time in stop-and-go lines. They cursed what appeared to be extra-long red lights, and particularly short green ones. And there was always someone ahead of them at the red lights who was oblivious to the change to green. Traffic seemed to be moving everywhere but in whichever lane Jack chose.

The Herties Tower was an impressive landmark. Jack had heard that they actually coated the glass with gold. Whether it served some special purpose, he was not sure. All he knew was that he could spot the building from every direction. Folks wanting to meet downtown made their plans with reference to the office tower, as in "two blocks north of the Herties building."

A lot of people didn't even bother with directions. They just arranged to meet at the tower and then walk, or drive, from there to wherever they were going.

Today it was Jack and Eric's turn. But once they got there, they intended to stay until their business was completed.

They parked the car in an underground lot two blocks away from the Herties Tower and walked among the shoppers and pedestrians, who were all hurrying to get to or from their various destinations.

The rain had started again. Jack and Eric ducked under the canopies of the businesses lining the sidewalk whenever they could and hurried through those spaces that did not offer cover.

The greatest challenge came at street corners, where they had to wait for the light to change. The trick was to hold back under a canopy or in a doorway until the light was about to change, and then move briskly out from under their cover and across the street without getting caught up in the traffic jam of humanity that seemed to form an immovable clot midstreet.

They soon arrived at the impressive facade of Mr. Herties' real estate empire. They were a little damper for their experience, but not so badly soaked that they might not be acceptable in the presence of a man who had the means to be confident he would never feel rain unless he wanted to.

Jack read the sign by the shining elevator door.

"We're going to the top," he announced to no one in particular.

"I gathered as much," Eric replied, assuming the comment was for his benefit.

The wait was longer than they had expected. The reason became obvious once the doors opened and the conveyance disgorged a mass of humanity that swarmed the lobby before moving out onto the street.

The two entered the coach, and Eric hit the topmost button. They were alone for the trip up and did not stop on the way. A soft whistle came from the doors as the elevator rocketed to its upper limit.

When they stepped out at their destination, it was apparent that there had been some sort of miscalculation. They were confronted by a hallway and a set of double glass doors. HERTIES ENTERPRISES ADMINISTRATION was written across their width in gold leaf. On the other side, they could see a counter and a pleasant-looking older woman, who was busying herself with what appeared to be a stack of files.

Jack pushed through the doors. Eric followed. The woman looked up from the documents she was inserting in the folders before her.

"Yes, gentlemen. How may I help you?" It appeared that her manner matched the initial impression Jack had formed.

"We are here to see Mr. Herties," he announced.

The woman laughed. Apparently looks can be deceiving. In an instant, she was not only all business, but had become the mother lion, protecting her cub.

"Mr. Herties sees no one without a prior appointment, and late Friday afternoons are the worst possible time to try to make one on short notice. I'm sorry, you can't . . ."

Jack wasn't in the mood. He cut her off midsentence. "We have some important information for Mr. Herties. It is imperative that we . . ."

"I'm sorry. You'll have to discuss things with him some other time." She was good at this game too.

"I think that if I could just have a moment of his time to explain my purpose in being here, he might give us an audience today."

"Sir, I have worked for Mr. Herties for twenty-eight years. I think I would know by now what he would and would not grant. Be assured that an unscheduled meeting is not something he would give you."

Jack was getting desperate. Something had to be done, and now. No use telling this woman that it was a personal matter. If she asked for details, Jack couldn't give them.

"May I use your phone? It's a local call."

"Yes, you can use that one." She pointed to a white phone on a table by the door. A reception area of sorts had been set up, with a couple of upholstered chairs and the table. Besides the phone, there were a number of business-oriented publications.

Jack sat, picked up the receiver, and listened. He reached into a pocket and pulled out a piece of paper. He dialed.

While he spoke, the woman returned to her filing. Every now and then, she would look up at Jack speaking into the receiver and pointedly look at her wristwatch.

Eric leaned against the wall beside Jack's chair, pretending not to hear the conversation. It sounded like the woman was about to be trumped.

Jack hung up.

"Thanks so much," he said, with such sincerity that even Eric was tempted to believe that all had been forgiven.

"You're quite welcome," said the woman, convinced.

"We'll only be here a few moments, and then we'll leave you alone."

She looked confused for a moment and then returned to her task.

Jack looked at Eric and smiled. "I want to see the look on her face," he whispered.

He didn't have long to wait. Moments later, the sound of elevator doors could be heard.

"He has a private entrance," Jack said quietly and indicated with a nod the far side of the office.

The receptionist was occupied with her filing and did not hear the approaching man. He was of medium height and lean. His hair was white, where he had hair. The top of his head was bald. He wore a dark blue suit.

"I hear these gentlemen were looking for me, Bett. I need to speak with them immediately."

The woman turned quickly. Her brow wrinkled. Her mouth dropped open. Her face took on a deep shade of pink.

"Mr. Herties . . . Sir, I . . . I'm sorry, sir. I didn't know you were expecting visitors."

"I wasn't. But now I am. Come with me, gentlemen."

Jack and Eric followed the man through the office to the waiting private elevator. The doors closed, leaving the confounded secretary behind.

"You'll have to forgive Bett. She tends to take her job quite seriously. That can be good, at the right times."

"She's only trying to protect you from unsavory types, and folks looking for a handout, I suspect," Jack offered.

Their host nodded and held out a hand to indicate they should exit the coach.

They found themselves in a lavish office with high ceilings and windows that occupied one entire wall. The view of the city was spectacular, or would have been, Jack thought, had it not been for the rain, which was launching a new assault.

"Sit down, please." Herties indicated well-upholstered leather chairs beside a desk that looked large enough to support a small dance band.

"Mr. Elton, you were mentioning on the phone that you had some information about my daughter." He leaned forward, fixing his eyes on Jack.

"I have some information, sir. It's not the best news you'll hear today. And I'm going to have to ask you to trust us, so that the news can get better."

"Is my daughter alright?" Panic showed in his eyes.

"Well, sir, I'm sure she is fine. But I suspect that she would be better if she were in different circumstances. Your daughter has been kidnapped."

There was no nice way to ease into the facts of the situation, and Jack was feeling the pressure of time. The kidnapper, whoever he was, had given Eric a deadline that they would have to take seriously, until there was some indication otherwise.

Jack continued. "We suspect that we have until sometime Monday to meet the kidnapper's demands. Somehow he has got a wrong number and thinks that he has been talking to you when, in fact, he has been calling my friend, Eric."

"I need to call the police about this." Mr. Herties was emphatic.

"I don't think that would be wise," Jack insisted. "The caller has told us that he does not want any indication that we—well, actually, *you*—have brought in the law. Strange as this may sound, that may be a good thing."

"How can that be?" The older man's voice trembled.

Herties' eyes pierced to Jack's soul as he leaned against the arm of his chair and ran his hand over what remained of the hair on top of his head.

"It's a fine point to be sure, but we are assuming that this guy will be watching you to see where you go—what you do. If you are seen in the company of your friend the chief, or if you make a trip to the police station, he will know you aren't playing ball with him. And you can't have the law coming here, either. We don't know how closely he is watching you."

"Is the good news coming somewhere in this explanation of yours, Mr. Elton?" Frustration showed on his face and in his voice now.

"Call me Jack, sir. Yes, there is a point to all this. You can't go to the police, but we can act as intermediaries.

"We are 'unknowns,' as far as this extortionist is concerned. He has been giving information to Eric here. We can pass that along to you and, with your help, can ask questions that might bring him out into the open and reveal his identity. If you agree to our plan, we can involve the police and not have it seem like you have tipped them off.

"Admittedly, I'm simplifying things, and we may be missing some major points, but we need to move quickly to get this under control. Eric has been holding the guy off, and so far the abductor has bought the story that you need time to get the cash together. By the way, he's asking for one million dollars for your daughter's return."

Herties blanched at Jack's last revelation but recovered quickly.

"Whatever the cost, I'll do whatever it takes to get Jennifer back. Tell me what you need me to do."

As the rain continued to fall and night rapidly approached, the three men huddled around the desk of the richest man in the city, if not the province or nation. Jack and Eric shared what they knew so far. Mr. Herties answered the questions they were asking to help with the deception they were planning, in hopes of saving the young girl.

"What process would you go through to get the money together?" Eric asked. "I want to sound like I know what I'm doing when this guy gets in touch again."

"You were wise to tell him that it would take time. It will," Herties replied. We have less time than we might have had, since his stupidity forced you to search me out. I can't forgive myself for waiting so long to try to find out why Jen hadn't called."

"Will the delay in finding you cause a problem with getting the money together for Monday?" Jack wanted to know.

"I can call my banker tonight. I have his private number, so I can call him at any time. I'll have to give him some sort of story to keep him from knowing what's going on. If I can't convince him, I can threaten. The chance that I might pull my account from his bank should soften his resolve. I'm willing to go to any lengths at all for my daughter."

Jack looked into the troubled face of a man who was learning that money can't buy happiness. This plan had to work if Jennifer Herties was to survive. He spoke with conviction.

"I might suggest that you go home tonight and inform your wife about all this. Let her know what we have talked about and help her to understand how important it is that she does not talk about this to anyone."

"That's easier said than done. Hennie is away visiting relatives in Germany. She's doing some traveling over in Europe, and I'm not sure how to contact her."

"That may be just as well," Jack said. "This might be a good case for 'what she doesn't know won't hurt her.' Hopefully by the time she hears anything, this whole nasty affair will be all over and resolved in your favor."

Herties grimaced. "For it to end any other way would be totally unacceptable," he said.

"We're going to do our best, sir. Now, can you think of anyone who might want to harm your daughter or take your money?"

Apparently there were many. Herties ordered in dinner, and they took the elevator to the boardroom one floor below to eat and continue their strategizing.

Chapter Six
Money Can't Buy Friends

"There was this one young man."

The dinner had been much more lavish than the sort of order-in fast food Jack and Eric were used to. They had packed away the bags and cartons for the cleaning staff that would come in later that night.

"Tell me about him," Jack asked.

"Jen and this guy—Byron. I think that was his name. Anyway, they had been going out for a while, and she dumped him."

"Lots of guys get dumped. Any reason this one comes to mind?" Jack was writing notes in a pad Mr. Herties had provided.

"He struck us—Hennie and me—as being a particularly manipulative type. Wanted Jen all to himself. Got all hot and bothered if she so much as looked at another boy. We had a few other candidates we would have preferred she date.

"Anyway, she got tired of his controlling nature and told him it was all over. Every now and then, he shows up in the picture, unannounced, and tries to get her back. She's been doing her best to ignore him."

"You think he's capable of pulling a stunt like this?" Jack asked.

"Wouldn't put it past him."

"Okay. We'll need a full name and address."

"I can get that for you when I get home," Herties responded. "I'm almost certain that his name is Byron.

"Of course, there was this other guy," he added. "He never made it to first base with Jen. He was a football player, on the varsity team. Jen was a cheerleader. She told us he used to look at her oddly when she had her uniform on. He tried to do things to impress her, but it worked against him. She hated him. Or so she said."

"We'll need his name too," Jack said, writing in his Herties notebook.

"I don't suppose you're interested in hearing about girls?" Herties looked from Jack to Eric and back again.

"Yes, sir. We want to know about anyone you think might be of interest to the police in this case. We'll want to talk to as many people as we can to try to bring this to a conclusion as soon as possible."

"Margaux Cox threatened her one time, when she lost the position of cheerleading captain to Jen." Herties was all business again.

"Snotty little kid. Thought the world owed her a living. Got a lot of attention because of her good looks. Personality like a wet tissue."

"Sounds delightful," Eric offered. His facial expression said otherwise.

"Yes, she was calling the house and threatening Jen with bodily harm. Had a nasty boyfriend wrapped around her little finger. She suggested he might do her dirty work."

"We'll have a little chat with Ms. Cox. That's for sure. We might talk to her little puppy too," Jack said with conviction.

"Now, here's a question that may be a little tougher to answer," he continued. "Is there anyone who might have something against you? Anyone you can think of who might be holding a grudge?"

It only took a moment. Herties shot forward in his seat, bending at the waist. His finger came up and pointed at Jack for emphasis.

"Fretz. Bernard Fretz. I fired him a couple of months ago. Of course, in my business there are probably hundreds of folks who would like to do me in. But yeah, he's the guy who comes immediately to mind. We still have his address and phone numbers on file. I can get those for you before you leave tonight."

Herties was showing signs of fatigue. He mopped his brow and moved the handkerchief over his face before stuffing it back in his pants pocket.

Jack decided that it was time to leave the man alone for a while and take what they had so they could plan their program. Like it or not, Jack Elton would be on the case for the weekend. It was time to get at it.

They got what contact information they could from Mr. Herties. He promised to call with the rest of the names and addresses to Jack as soon as possible.

"I hope you'll forgive me if I make a few inquiries around town, gentlemen. We've never met, and in my business I need to be sure that I'm not making wrong decisions. I'm willing to trust you, Jack, just as long as you turn out to be who you say you are."

"Well, sir," Jack replied, "you may find a skeleton or two in my old locker at the police station. But talk to Ted Brown. He should be able to put your mind at ease, at least a little."

"We all have things in our lives that haunt us," Herties said. "But solve this thing to my satisfaction, and I'll show my appreciation. If I feel that things are going too slowly, all bets are off, and I'll have to consider other means of dealing with this."

"I appreciate your vote of confidence, sir. I'll try not to let you down. Eric is going to pretend to be you for a while longer. You concentrate on getting the money. We'll do everything to make sure you get it all back."

Herties called down to the security desk in the lobby to let the guard know that two strangers would be leaving. He escorted Jack and Eric to the elevator and used a key to give them access. They said their farewells, and the two men took their trip to the main floor.

"Good evening gentlemen." A balding man in a blue police uniform greeted them when the elevator doors opened. A name tag announced BARNES SECURITY— RANDALL AUSTIN.

"Good evening, Officer Austin. Lovely evening," Jack said enthusiastically. "We're on our way out."

"You can have it," Austin replied. "Lousy night, weather-wise. Great for water fowl."

He let them out of the building, and they walked along to the underground parking to pick up Jack's car. Jack and Eric went down dimly lit stairs that smelled of a mixture of mold, urine, and old beer. Jack's car was easy enough to find. Most folks had headed home a long time ago and, except for those few who still had business or pleasure in the city, the garage was almost empty.

Jack's tires squealed as he drove around and up the ramps that led eventually to the little kiosk by the exit. There, a totally uninterested woman with wild hair and her nose in a paperback snatched the parking stub from Jack and ran it through a scanner.

"That'll be six bucks," she said, her hand extended.

"Here ya go," Jack said, handing bills and coins to the attendant.

She closed her fist, punched a button, and returned to her reading. The gate across the exit opened. Jack drove up the ramp to the street.

"And a pleasant evening to you too," he said once the window was cranked up and they were on the street. He gave Eric a quick glance.

"I'll drive you back to your place. Maybe our guy has called. Let me know when you get in. Call my cell. I may be out tracking some things down."

"Or you may be conferring with a certain cop," Eric said with a smile.

"That's a possibility, but my mind will be on the business at hand tonight, I'm afraid. We'll see."

They drove on in silence to Eric's apartment building. Jack pulled up to the front entry and stopped.

"We've got a whole lot of work ahead of us this

weekend, if we're going to get this over with by Monday," he said, turning on the dome light.

"You remember that too," Eric said. "Don't stay up too late this evening. Let's plan to get an early start on things."

"Check your answering machine the moment you get in. Call my cell if you've heard from our phantom. If you are speaking to him, play it cool. Remember what Herties told you. And make notes of anything that might help. Talk to you later."

Eric pulled the door handle, stepped out, and closed the door. He patted the roof a couple of times and called through the closed window, "Drive safely."

"Thanks," Jack called back and drove off.

It wasn't quite nine yet. Jack picked up his cell phone and dialed a number. He spoke briefly to the young woman on the other end, hung up, and dialed the number he had just been given.

"Hi. Sorry to bother you so close to closing. I was there earlier this afternoon. I'm with the police," he lied. "Well, I'm looking for some information about a few of your students. No, as far as I know, they are not in any trouble with the law. I just need you to verify some names for me."

The young man at the other end of the line was obviously more trusting, or less strongly indoctrinated in the ways of personal privacy law. He checked the names for Jack and reported his findings.

Jack folded the phone and felt for the small well in the console between the seats. He dropped the phone in.

"How can that be possible?" he asked himself out loud,

as he tried to see through the sheen of water that his wipers couldn't seem to clear completely. "How can they not be registered at the university? There must be something I am missing."

The wet road made his headlights almost ineffective. The reflection from streetlights and oncoming traffic obliterated any signs of the center line.

Jack slowed down. No use rushing to get into an accident. He fished out the phone again. He dialed Valerie's number. He had to see her tonight. He regretted that it would be all business. There was just too much that needed to be done.

He finally arrived at the apartment block and made sure to park in a well-lit area. The failure to take that precaution in the past had resulted in some serious damage to the old car he had once owned and, in one case, some serious physical damage that had ended his police career. Of course, there had been other circumstances that helped him off the force. He tried to put that out of his mind. He has a new life now.

When Valerie opened her apartment door, she was met by a thoroughly damp Jack Elton. He hated hats, and the rain didn't care. His hair was slicked down, and his beige coat was stained dark by the water.

She helped him out of the wet garment and handed him some towels to dry off with. Jack spent some time in her bathroom getting sorted out.

When he returned, Valerie retrieved the wet towels and tossed them in a hamper by a small washer. The apartment felt warm, and Jack was feeling the chill come off already.

Valerie had prepared hot chocolate. They sat across from one another as Jack reviewed his afternoon for her.

"What I can't understand is why there is no record of the Herties girl, or her friends, at the university. Unless I'm mistaken, Jennifer has been studying here. Her father specifically mentioned her course in leadership. I think he said she was going for a master's degree."

"There's where you went wrong," Valerie said, smiling at Jack. There is more than one school in town. Not everybody goes to UBC."

"I never thought of that."

"The leadership course is specific to Vantage Community College, west of here. I'll bet that's where you'll find your girl and her friends registered. Some of them, anyway. Vantage doesn't have a football team and, obviously, no cheerleading squad.

"It's apparent that some of the problems she had were during her years at another school. If not UBC, maybe somewhere else. I think her father will be able to help you there. You're getting rusty with your interrogations. A good cop would have verified information rather than jump to a conclusion. Aren't you glad you have me around to help?" Valerie smiled.

Jack felt warmer inside. *Back to business,* he thought.

"Back to business," he said. "I'm not quite sure where to start with the leads Herties gave. There's a guy who has it in for him, but there is a cartload of people who either don't like him or would like his money. Then there are Jen's friends. There seems to be so much to do in such a short period of time."

"Bird by bird," she said.

"Just what is that supposed to mean?" Jack asked.

"A friend of mine is reading a book by this writer who had a school assignment when she was young. It was a book report on birds, but there were so many of them, she didn't know where to start, so she asked her dad. He told her that the best way to get through her list was to do it bird by bird. So that's what she did."

"I think I get it," Jack said. "You are saying that the simplest thing to do is just start with one and go through the list."

"Yeah, something like that. Just pick a name. Do an interview and move on. Once you've asked all your questions, hopefully you'll be closer to some answers."

"Aren't we logical tonight?" Jack said.

Valerie smiled, and Jack's thermostat turned up another notch. He waited while she prepared some more hot chocolate for them.

"I want to get some extracurricular support from your colleagues this weekend. Anything possible there?"

"I'll see what I can do," she said. "You're probably not going to like this, but your friend is on this weekend."

"Willis the weasel."

"The very same. But don't be so harsh. I think he's getting to like you."

"He's okay as a cop, but sometimes his attitude just gets to me," Jack said.

"Yeah. Keegan Willis gets on my nerves at times, too, but he's a good cop. He means well. I just think maybe he doesn't have such a high opinion of himself."

"Should he?"

Valerie ignored the question and pressed on. "Besides Keegan there's Brown."

"Now you're talking."

Chief Detective Ted Brown was a guy who knew how to handle police work. Jack would have been willing to trust his life to the head of the detective division. Brown acted as a buffer between the ex-cop and Willis, who was known for going by the book to the distraction of those around him. Jack had begun to believe that his nemesis had memorized the book.

"That's all I know for sure. Detective division got the same heads-up as the patrol officers. Ears to the ground. Nothing too specific," Val said.

"Do they know what we know?"

"I don't think so. Not yet. I thought you'd want to share your plan with them first."

"Our plan, you mean. You were the one who figured out we could bring them in to this thing, as long as they didn't show up anywhere around Mr. Herties," Jack said. "By the way, he'll be fully on board with the plan. For some reason, he's willing to trust me to handle this, provided I pass his initial scrutiny."

"That's good. I don't like the idea of you and Eric going at this like the Lone Ranger and his sidekick. And I'm not saying that just because I'm a police officer."

"Does this mean you care?" Jack asked with a wink.

"Yes, you silly man. I care."

Jack and Valerie continued to work late into the evening. From time to time he called Eric to ask if there was any news from Jen's abductor. There had been none. The results of their consultation were a list of suspects and a plan for approaching them and interrogating everyone about their relationship, past and present, with Jennifer Herties.

Jack hated to leave, but he knew if he stayed much longer, his good resolve would crumble, and business would turn into pleasure. He had to be rested and prepared for a busy weekend. There was no telling when another call would come that would change things for him, Eric, and Valerie, and for Jennifer.

"Let's plan to meet up tomorrow morning, at about eight. We'll start our rounds and try to get as much done as possible before noon," he suggested.

"Looks like our meeting will be later today. It's after midnight," Val said. "Let's hope something comes to light—no pun intended—by midday."

They embraced, and Jack shrugged on his coat, which had almost dried in the warmth of Valerie's apartment. He took the elevator down and walked out to his car.

Jack drove directly to his apartment. The rain had stopped. Maybe the day ahead would be brighter than the last, in more ways than one.

Jack prepared for bed quickly and went into his bedroom. He lay down on his bed and slept where he fell, until the ringing of his phone roused him.

Chapter Seven
Saturday—Up and At 'Em

Jack's sleep had been so profound that he didn't quite catch the call before the answering machine began its announcement. *"I'm not available right now. I may be on the other line. If you would like to leave a message . . ."*

Jack didn't have another line. He snatched up the receiver.

"Hello." He was surprised at the hoarseness of his own voice. A mixture of fatigue and a day of rain was obviously contributing to the raspiness.

"Hi, Jack." Eric sounded in an exuberant mood. He had been the fortunate one who got the extra hours of sleep, once Jack had quit calling, the previous evening.

"Hi, Eric. I'm on my way. I was just heading out."

"Just heading out of bed is more like it. Don't worry. You haven't missed anything. I just thought I'd call in case you needed a little prodding to get up. Sounds like my instincts were right."

"You're all heart, my friend. Valerie is coming to get me at about eight. You'll need your own car today, because we may have to be in a few places at once.

"You know where we had breakfast the other day? We'll plan to meet there about quarter past. We'll have a quick run-down of the day's activities and then head out to do our work. I'll need you for a while this morning. Then I'm going to ask you to baby-sit your phone. If our guy calls when you are out, he'll have to call back. I want you to put a new message on your answering machine, assuring callers that you will be back at noon and that they should call back. I want you to identify your place as the Herties residence.

"It occurred to me, late last night, that your answering machine just says, 'Hi, I'm not in,' and all that stuff about how important the call is to you. We're fortunate our guy hasn't called while you were out so far. He might have started to believe you were telling the truth when you said you weren't Mr. H."

"I'll get on it right away," Eric said. "Now, you get dressed and wait for the cop. I'll see you at Timmie's."

Forty-five minutes later, the three were sitting at a table in the doughnut shop. Valerie had been right on time, and Jack had only been another five minutes getting ready. Eric had been waiting for them when they entered.

"Here's the deal," Jack said when everyone had had a chance to settle and drink some coffee. "Herties called just before Val arrived and gave me some more details about the folks we are going to be talking to."

"What did you want me to do this morning?" Eric asked.

"I've got a special assignment for you. I'll get to that in just a moment. Val and I are going to see Margaux Cox. She's the only female, for the time being, at least. I don't want any suggestions of impropriety at this stage of the game. I need another female present. Maybe Val can ask the questions, and I'll play stenographer."

Eric smiled and winked at Valerie. "You'll look good in panty hose, Jack," he said.

"Let's try to stay serious for a moment." Jack was obviously feeling the tension of the situation and had temporarily lost his usual sense of humor.

"Eric, here is what I'd like you to do. You are going to talk to Byron Leach. He's a former boyfriend. You're going to pretend to be a family acquaintance. You'll call him first. If he sounds like our guy, or if you have any reservations about him, let me know. We'll call in the cavalry.

"Valerie and I are going to become an aunt and uncle of Jennifer Herties'. We can't reach the family, and we're trying to find our niece. We'll have to play the rest by ear."

"You realize how dangerous this all is, don't you, Jack?" Valerie's serious expression was alarming to both of the men. "Aren't you afraid that whoever the culprit is will get suspicious of family or friends asking pointed questions?"

"It's a chance were going to have to take. Time is short," Jack said. "We don't have the luxury of being able to beat around the bush. We have to be able to make it appear that Jen's dad has not called in the police. In fact, he hasn't. We did."

"Do you really think that's going to make a whole lot of difference to this guy?" Valerie asked.

"I'm hoping that we catch on to him before he catches on to us. If he decides to take any decisive action, we will hopefully be able to prevent Jen from getting hurt. It's a certainty she'll be dead if we don't do anything. Dad can afford the ransom, but we can't be sure that this guy won't try to get rid of his hostage once he has the cash."

Valerie looked doubtful.

"Shall we give this a try?" Jack asked.

After a few more instructions, Eric headed off to track down Byron Leach. He had the phone number and address that Mr. Herties had given Jack early that morning.

Eric sat in his car and dialed. Jack and Valerie could see him talking as they headed across the parking lot toward her vehicle.

They were on their way out of the lot when Eric waved them to stop. They pulled alongside, and Jack rolled down his window.

"This is what I've got so far," Eric reported. "He lives with his parents still. I talked to his mom. He's home. Still asleep. He was out late last night. I'm going to take a chance and drive over to the west side to meet him. If he's our guy, I can't see him acting up right there, in front of Mummy and Daddy."

"You just be careful," Jack called through the open car window. "Keep your phone on, and call me if you sense trouble. We'll get Keegan and Ted involved, if we have to."

"I'll be okay," Eric replied. With that, he pulled out of the lot and headed west.

Jack and Valerie headed east, to the affluent part of town. The sun had risen above the horizon formed by the skyline of the city. The rain of the previous evening was becoming just a memory. A bright, blue fall sky appeared to be held up by the spire that marked the top of the Herties building.

It was just nine when Jack and Valerie crossed the bridge into the business section of town. They continued to the east and watched as high rises gave way to manicured lawns and well-tended gardens. Steel and glass were replaced by brick and stone and imported wood. A higher class of neighbor lived in this community. As Jack thought about it, he realized that all these folks had money, but only some had real class. He wondered which assessment best suited the family of Ms. Margaux Cox.

It was a massive edifice that greeted Jack and Valerie, as they drove up the long drive. The house was stone. The semicircular roadway led to a main entrance with heavy wooden doors framed by marble columns. Windows on either side gave only a glimpse of the luxury that the Cox family found possible.

Jack stopped the car in front of the house, got out, and went to Valerie's side to open her door.

"Gotta keep up appearances, Aunt Val," he whispered as he helped her out.

Jack and Valerie were ushered into the house by a maid who had answered the doorbell. The servant wore street clothes and carried a dust cloth in one hand.

"Miss Margaux will be with you shortly. Please take a seat in the family room."

She led them to a large open space with deep-pile carpeting and furniture that neither Jack nor Valerie could ever hope of affording. She left them alone, polishing fingerprints off the doorknob as she went. After a while, they could hear a vacuum cleaner in the distance.

"I'm not convinced that this suspect needs the cash. Let's see if she might want revenge."

Valerie hushed him.

"We'll talk about this later, dear. Remember, we are looking for our niece."

"Sorry. Almost forgot. Thanks for the reminder. Lovely place," Jack said, affecting an upper-class British accent.

"Yes, it is. A little too expensive for me, I'm afraid. Jen has some fortunate friends," Val said.

They fell silent and waited. Margaux Cox's clock obviously ran a lot slower than most folks'.

Jack stood and occupied himself looking at the paintings on the wall. The Cox family didn't waste their money on cheap prints. Margaux was probably well cared for. Herties thought she was spoiled. *We'll see,* Jack thought.

The "shortly" the maid had spoken of was twenty minutes. Margaux entered the room wearing shorts and a T-shirt. It was a combination that barely contained her well-shaped posterior and her amply endowed chest. She had auburn hair that hung loose to her waist and a smile that would win contests and probably influence people. Valerie noticed Jack's immediate attention to these details.

"Like, hi there. I'm Margaux, but my friends call me Mar. You're, like, Jen's, like, aunt and uncle?"

"Yeah, something like that," Valerie replied.

"We're trying to find her, but her dad hasn't heard from her for a while," Jack added.

"Bummer!" the girl said with apparent sincerity.

Jack continued. "Do you have any idea where she might be?"

"No. Jen and I don't talk much anymore. We used to be friends and then we, like, had a fight, like, and I haven't seen her in ages. 'Course, I haven't been looking much." She smiled and tossed her hair, which had fallen over one eye.

Jack had to try to remember his fake persona as he spoke, for fear of giving away the real reason he was asking his questions.

"Musta been a big fight. Over a boy, was it?"

"Oh my gosh, no. It was about two years ago. We were trying out for the cheerleading squad. She beat me out for the last spot. I think I deserved that place on the team. It wasn't fair."

Jack would not have been surprised if she had stamped her foot at this point. She was winding up for a tantrum. It needed to be nipped in the bud.

"I'm sorry to hear that you couldn't both be on the squad. You're still a little angry after all this time."

"I know how you feel," Valerie began. "If it were me, I'd be really angry. I'd want to get back at her."

"Not me," Margaux said convincingly enough. "That was last year. Sometimes I'm sorry we stopped being friends. At the time, I said I wanted to kill her, but I didn't really mean it. We had such good times together."

A wistful look crossed the face of the girl who could probably have any boy she wanted, and could buy anything else.

She continued. "Funny. Mrs., um . . ."

"Herties. Valerie Herties." She had to lie, and hoped

she and Jack would be able to carry off the deception for a while longer.

"So you must be W. D.'s brother," Margaux said.

"Something like that." Jack smiled his best smile at the young girl.

"I'm really sorry to hear you can't find Jen. She's got to be around town somewhere. I think she's, like, taking courses out at the community college. Have you been out there? Maybe she's, like, got an exam she's studying for?"

Margaux had a habit of sometimes making her statements sound like questions.

"We'll have to give that a try," Val said. "Come on, Jack. Let's take a trip out there. That's probably where she is."

"What? Oh, right. Sure," Jack said, gathering his thoughts again. "That's probably where she is. I guess we'll be moving along for now."

"It's been good talking to you, Mar," he added. "Maybe you and Jen will patch things up one of these days."

Jack was surprised to see a tear forming in the girl's eye.

"Yeah, that would be so cool," Margaux said, making a quick swipe at her eyes with a fingertip.

She escorted them to the door, and they said their good-byes. Jack and Valerie got into the car and completed the circuit of the driveway, which brought them back onto the street.

"Well, that was a complete waste of time," Jack said. His face showed the regret he was feeling.

"Not every lead is going to be a gem. You know that. Some people just don't have anything to add to the mix," Valerie assured him.

"Anyway, it wasn't a complete loss," she added. "I

think we can strike her off the list for now. And you seemed to enjoy looking at her."

A pink flush made Jack's face feel warm in the cool air inside the car.

"I'll have to admit, it was hard to look her straight in the eye. But remember, as far as those things go, I only have eyes for you." It was Jack's turn to give assurances.

"Yeah. I hope you picked them up off the floor before we left."

Jack didn't reply. He considered himself well chastised.

He was quiet as he reflected on the conversation they had had with the girl. As he drove, he asked, "What's the W. D. stand for?"

"Where?" Valerie looked out the window to see where he was talking about.

"Not there, back at the house. Mar said that I must be W. D.'s brother. She must have meant Herties. What do the letters stand for?"

"Darned if I know. But you're right. I've only ever heard of him referred to as W. D. Herties. Could be William David or Winston Daniel or . . ."

"Or Whoopee Ding," Jack joked.

"Very funny. I don't suppose it matters, really. It's the way he likes to be known. No big deal."

"Way Decadent," Jack added.

"Let's not let this go on too long, shall we." Valerie reached over and patted the side of his face.

Chapter Eight
Places to Go, People To See

They drove on toward the perimeter of the city and the suburbs beyond.

They stopped for lunch at an old pub that had been a stopping place in the days of the horse and buggy. Lately it had been converted into a restaurant that was known for ample servings at reasonable prices.

They were shown to a corner table and settled in while they waited for the menu.

After their orders had been taken, Jack excused himself and stepped outside. He pulled out his cell phone and made a call. He returned to the table as the waiter was bringing their order.

For a while, they ate in silence. The food was tasty and hot.

Finally Jack said, "It is all arranged. We'll meet at Vantage Community College this afternoon and look for clues. Herties will meet us there. W. D.'s making arrangements for us to get into Jen's dorm room."

"Ah, so now we're on a first-letter basis with the richest man in town."

"Hush. You want the bill for this to skyrocket?" Jack warned with a smile.

"You think we ought to see how Eric is making out?" Val asked.

"I'll call him as soon as we're finished here. You want dessert?"

They decided to pass up the sweet stuff in favor of getting on with the work at hand. The bill was eventually presented, and Jack left payment in cash to avoid the delay that using a credit card would create.

Outside again, he stood in the parking lot and dialed Eric's cell number.

The phone was answered on the first ring.

"Hi, Jack. I've been out to visit the boyfriend, or rather ex-boyfriend. Interesting situation, there. Mom swore he was still asleep. She knocked on the bedroom door. We talked for a while, and he was still a no-show. She finally went into his room and discovered he wasn't there.

"I won't go into the song and dance I had to endure about how he must have slipped out earlier in the morning. Suffice it to say, by the looks of the room, he didn't come home last night. I can fill you in later. What do you want right now?"

"Right now, I want you back at your apartment," Jack answered. "If our guy calls, I want you to be able to assure him that you, W. D. Herties, are working on getting the money together."

"Yeah, I have a hard time remembering who I'm supposed to be. I'm one guy this morning, and another this afternoon. I'm starting to feel schizophrenic. Are those his initials, W. D.?"

"I know it sounds funny, but this is serious business. Don't let your guard down for a moment. Answer your phone as Herties all afternoon. And his initials are W. D., yes. Just discovered that myself."

"What's your plan for the afternoon?" Eric asked.

Jack leaned on the roof of the car with both elbows as he held the phone to one ear.

"Val and I have an appointment with the real W. D. We're meeting him at Vantage Community College. He's going to get us into Jen's residence so we can look for clues. I'll let you know how successful that is later on. Call me if you get anything you think might be helpful, like a call from the guy who's got Jennifer."

"Okay, Jack. I sure hope we can do something helpful."

"Don't worry, Eric, we're on the case. Something will come of all this."

Jack was careful not to suggest whether what came of it might be good or bad. He hung up and slid into the driver's seat beside Valerie.

"Looks like Herties and Herties are both on the case," he said and started the engine.

They drove along the highway amid Saturday afternoon traffic. The lines were long in both directions as folks from the city headed for the stores in the suburbs, and those from out of town headed for the malls in the city.

Jack was thankful that their trip would not be a long one. The stop-and-go traffic got on his nerves, and he was anxious to check out a possible scene of the crime.

"What's the news from Eric?" Valerie asked, not taking her eyes off traffic.

"I think we should keep an eye on Byron. He wasn't where he was supposed to be, and his parents couldn't give any explanation. Could be he's off somewhere tending to his hostage. I told Eric to go home and wait for a call. Maybe we'll get some more information from this guy."

They drove up the hill to the college. Jack swung into the entrance to the campus. They passed the stone gates and followed the winding drive that led to a visitors' parking lot.

They walked the short distance toward the students' residence and stopped across from the castle-like structure that housed the college's classrooms and library. The building was a major feature of travel brochures and the school's publicity pieces. It had been the site of movie shoots and fancy dress balls. It added a fairy tale atmosphere to the campus.

Jack was surprised to notice that the car that finally delivered Mr. Herties was a regular midsized sedan and not a fancy limousine.

Tipping his chin in the direction of the vehicle, he commented to Valerie, "I guess he tries to avoid being noticed as much as possible. I see that he didn't drive himself, though."

"When you're as rich and well known, as he is, it's probably best not to draw too much attention to yourself.

And now that it appears as if someone is out to cause him some grief, I'd image he would want to keep a low profile," Valerie replied.

The multimillionaire had stepped out of the car by then and came along the walkway toward them. Jack approached without looking Herties in the eye.

Under his breath, Jack said, "I'm not sure who's watching, pretend we've just met," and stuck out his hand to the gentleman.

"Excuse me, sir, I'm Jack and this is my friend Valerie. You're W. D. Herties, aren't you?"

"Why, yes, I am. How do you like the campus?"

"It's a beautiful place. I'm just sorry we can't look around inside."

"Come with me. Jack, is it? And Valerie? Follow me. I'll give you a little tour."

Without further comment, Herties stepped along the sidewalk, and the other two followed behind. Jack ran up the stairs to the residence to get ahead of the older man. He opened and held the door. Herties motioned Valerie to go first. As he passed Jack, he whispered, "Well done. Well done, indeed."

Once inside, Jack and Valerie held back while Herties spoke in hushed tones with the security guard in a little booth to one side.

The guard picked up a phone and pushed some numbers. He listened, then hung up the phone with a shake of his head.

After a few more moments of discussion, the guard pulled out a book and laid it open on the counter before the visitor. He presented him with a pen. Herties signed and held out the pen for Jack.

"Here you go, Jack. I've been explaining to this nice man that you and Valerie are relatives from out of town who have come to see where Jen lives. He tells me that Jen isn't here right now. She doesn't answer her intercom, but it would be a shame for you to come all this way and not be able to see as much of the campus as possible."

He introduced Jack as his nephew and Valerie as Jack's girlfriend. Jack signed, "J. Herties."

Valerie signed with her real name. She was aware of her obligation as a peace officer and could use the registration as proof of her own honesty, if called to do so.

"Where ya from?" the guard asked, looking at Jack.

"Regina," Val replied.

"Nice place."

"Sure is."

Herties ushered them away from the cubicle and into the stairwell. They went as quickly as possible to the floor that held Jennifer's room and, they hoped, some clues to her whereabouts.

"Typical dorm room," Jack said after Herties finally got the key to work in the old lock.

"Just like mine when I went to college," Valerie added.

A single bed had been placed along one wall, head toward the window, which looked out onto the woods at the back of the residence. A desk was built into the wall opposite. There was a fluorescent tube under a bookcase suspended over the desk. Some of Jen's books were piled on the work surface. Others were lined up on the shelves.

The bed was made, and some sort of sleepwear was folded beside the pillow.

"See anything that might be helpful?" the father asked.

"Nothing jumps out for immediate attention," Valerie answered, her trained eyes scanning the room.

"There's a diary here," Jack said, looking at the pile of books on the desk. "Maybe it will offer us a clue to your daughter's whereabouts. Will you give us permission to look?"

"Certainly. Is there any doubt about that?" The man sounded offended.

"It's not that, sir. It's just that we want to do this as legally as possible. There may be occasion to do some things that might not gain the approval of the law, as we work through this. I want to do as much as possible in an appropriate manner.

"Valerie, I'll let you do the honors. You're the one with the badge—somewhere," Jack said.

"It's still at home, on my uniform. Okay, let's have a look."

Valerie opened the book carefully and began gingerly turning pages.

"Not much here. Just the regular girl stuff. She had an exam in business ethics last week. Went out for lunch with some friends. There's a professor she's not too fond of. Mostly just assignments and a record of her day-to-day activities.

"Here's something interesting. She was going out with some friends on Wednesday. Dinner and drinks. Doesn't say where. The entries end there. I wonder if she came back home that night or . . ."

"She didn't."

The voice at the door belonged to an undernourished-looking girl with rusty hair in braids. A few strands had come loose and made her look somewhat frayed. She walked into the room and stuck out her right hand.

"I'm Sara. I was with Jen the other night. We went out to the pub down the road. We were there till about eleven thirty."

"Was Jennifer with you the whole time?" Jack asked. Valerie and Herties showed obvious interest as well.

"Yep. Right up until almost the end."

"She didn't come back here with you?" Valerie asked.

"We were all set to leave when she got a phone call. She looked properly ticked. Uh, I'm sorry. She was rather put out by whatever the message was. She said she'd be back later.

"We came back here. There were three of us. But she never showed."

"Didn't that make you wonder where she had got to?" Jack asked.

"Not really. She's a big girl. We went to bed eventually. Figured she'd be along at some point," Sara said.

"I figure she came back and left early for class, or the library, on Thursday. We don't have classes together so I didn't see her all day. She probably went home for the weekend. You family?"

"You might say that," Jack said.

"I'll let her know you were here, when I see her," Sara assured them, unaware of the peril her friend might be in.

The girl disappeared down the hall. Jack heard coins

being inserted into a vending machine in the distance, followed by the *thunk* of a pop can falling into the dispenser chute.

"We've got to try to find out what the phone call was about and who it was from," Herties said to the other two.

Jack looked to Valerie for a response but only got a barely perceptible shake of the head.

"I think that would help us a great deal," Jack said, thinking to himself that it was probably the key to the whole thing.

They continued their survey of the small room. There was only the one room. Clothes were hung on a rack behind the door. They had seen the common bathrooms as they came along the hall earlier.

"I guess there isn't much else here," Herties offered with a shrug. His voice showed his frustration and fear for his daughter's life.

"We were fortunate to have that brief encounter with Jen's friend. It's obvious, though, that she hasn't any more information to offer at the moment. I guess we can move on, then," Jack said.

He went toward the door as he spoke. Valerie put the diary back on the desk. Herties looked less and less the multimillionaire, and more the worried father, with each passing moment.

He thanked the security man by the door and entered the time out for the three of them.

The trio stepped out into the lengthening shadows of the autumn afternoon and headed toward the roadway.

Herties' driver saw their approach and drove up from

where he was parked. He waited in the car while Jack and Valerie said their farewells to his boss.

"I appreciate your coming with me this afternoon," Herties said as they stood by the road.

"Well, thank you for letting us poke around in there. We didn't find much, but at least there was no sign of a struggle, so we can assume that your daughter was not abducted from her room," Jack said.

"That hardly seems like much," Herties replied.

"Everything helps at a time like this. I would suspect that Jennifer knows whoever it is who has taken her. We'll hope that that familiarity will help us in getting her back. We also have the detail that Sara gave us while we were up there," Jack added. "I think we can assume Jen was enticed to go somewhere, to meet whoever it was."

"Tell me honestly, do you think you can sort this all out before it's too late?" Herties asked.

"We'll just have to, sir. It can't be any other way," Jack replied with a conviction he wasn't sure he could back up.

"Call me, at any hour. You have my private cell number. Here's my home phone as well." He reached in his jacket pocket and pulled out a card, which he offered to Jack.

"Thank you, sir," Jack said. "I'll keep you informed of anything we learn. I hope it's also all right if we need to ask you some questions."

"That will be just fine. I'll be waiting for your call."

With that, he strode to the car. The chauffeur was out of his seat and holding the door before he had got two steps from the other two. The door closed, and the driver settled in. They drove up the hill and onto the street beyond the gates.

Jack and Valerie started to walk down to the parking lot. Jack looked at the card that Herties had given him.

"Well, I'll be darned. Look at that, will ya."

He handed the card to Valerie, who stared at it, turned it over, and went to hand it back.

"It's his business card. What of it?" she asked.

"Look again." Jack had a knowing grin on his face. He raised his eyebrows as Valerie took another look.

"I must be dense, I don't see anything."

"Look at the phone number. Look closely."

"One of the numbers is blurred. So what?" Val asked.

"Not blurred, my dear. Written over. It was a nine, but an eight has been penned over it."

Valerie stopped walking and turned to look at Jack.

"And . . ." she said.

"And the difference between his number and Eric's is that one digit. I wonder when W. D. realized his stationer had made a mistake. I wonder if someone might have got an uncorrected card and is using it to try to contact Herties."

"I wonder if Mr. Herties has his cell phone on," Valerie said.

Chapter Nine
Round and Round We Go

The now familiar voice of W. D. Herties answered Jack's call to his cell phone. They had only said their good-byes a few moments ago.

"I hope you don't think this an unusual question, sir, but I need to ask you about that business card you gave me before you left." Jack hoped that the answers he got might begin to unlock some of the mysteries surrounding all that had been happening over the past three days.

"Fire away, son. No harm in asking, and deep regret over questions that should have been answered but were never asked."

Jack's face brightened at the response.

"I noticed that there was apparently an error in the printing of your home number. On my card, it has been changed in pen. It was a nine, but an eight has been penned over it."

"That is correct. It's my turn to wonder if you'll think me strange," the millionaire replied.

"Indeed, the number was printed incorrectly," he continued. "I know it doesn't look good for someone who should be able to afford to pay for replacements to use a pen. I did have new ones made. In fact, the printer did the job at no cost. I keep those new corrected ones in my desk.

"I'm a bit of an environmentalist, even though I am accused of tearing down trees to build some of my developments. I hated to see all those cards end up in the garbage, so I carry the misprinted ones in my jacket, and correct with a pen as I go."

"It's very important you try to tell me how long it took for you to notice the error," Jack said.

There was a pause as Mr. Herties apparently searched the aging memory banks for the answer.

"Let me see. The cards were delivered back in September. The first week, I think," he finally answered.

"They would have come to my office, and Bett would have signed for them. She left them on my desk, and I didn't give them much thought. I started giving them out about a week later. I gave some to staff. Bett would have included some in mail we sent out. That's how I found out about it. Bett came steaming into the office one morning and pointed it out. She said she had already talked to the stationer. Well, you know what a force she can be. That's how I got the new ones. I would say it was about three days after I first started distributing them."

Jack could hear the sounds of the car as it ferried Herties to his next destination.

"The reason I ask, sir, is because it seems that one of the folks who got a card before you started correcting them used the incorrect number. That's how my friend was mistaken for you. That's how we find ourselves in this peculiar relationship we have developed."

"Interesting. Do you think that might be useful?" Herties asked.

"I think it might help us narrow the field somewhat. Give me some time to work on things, and we'll see where it leads."

"That's quite a head you have on your shoulders, Jack. I'm feeling a little more hopeful that you can solve this whole thing."

"Thank you, sir." Jack hung up. He held the car door for Valerie, then walked around to the driver's side and got in.

"I wish I had as much faith in me as he does," he said, starting the engine and putting the car in gear.

"Do you think this thing about the phone number is really going to help?" Val asked.

"That's what he asked. I'm not sure, but if it turns just the right way, we could use it to catch our man. Let's see if Eric has any news."

Jack dialed the number and was greeted by the voice of his friend.

"Herties here."

"Hi Eric, it's only me. Anything new this afternoon?"

"As a matter of fact, yeah."

Jack's eyebrows rose significantly, and he nodded as if his friend could see the indication to proceed.

"It was rather short and sweet. I didn't get an opportunity to say anything. He did all the talking," Eric said.

"What did he say?"

Valerie heard the question and fixed her eyes on Jack.

"It was along the lines of 'Make sure you get the cash by Monday. Remember, I'm watching you, so stay away from the cops, and they had better stay away from you.' "

"Anything about the girl?" Jack asked.

"All he said was she was alive and well, and nothing had happened to her yet. He made sure to make it sound ominous."

"He believed you?" Jack signaled for a right turn that would take him and Valerie back toward town.

"He didn't give any indication that he thought otherwise."

"Good. I think we have a little bit of valuable information. I know why you are the one who is getting the calls."

"Really?" Eric asked.

"Yeah. I'll tell you the next time I see you. It probably won't be tonight. I've got other things on my mind."

"That's okay with me. I've got a date with a lovely lady myself. I'm sure I'll have other things on my mind too," Eric said.

"Just be careful how you answer the phone. And your date can't know anything about what we've been doing lately. You may want to reconsider that date."

"Don't worry, Jack. I can handle things just fine."

"You'd better hang up, Jack," Valerie said. "The traffic is starting to get a little heavier. We don't want to have an accident."

Jack concluded his conversation with Eric and put the cell phone away.

"Thanks for the warning, Officer," he said with a smile.

They drove on without speaking. The autumn sun setting behind them gave a golden hue to the scenery. It reminded Jack of the tower that dominated the city skyline and the man whose name was emblazoned above its doors.

Those who saw the Herties Tower would think that the man had not a care in the world, and that he could buy happiness.

Boy, are they wrong, Jack thought. As he drove he contemplated the new details that had been brought to light. Somehow they all fit together and explained one another. Perhaps it was time to talk to the professionals.

"Maybe we should swing around to your office and talk to the folks in the detective division. I want to run some things by them. You don't mind a little extra police work, do you?" he asked Val.

"I suppose not. I'd only worry about that poor girl if I was at home, and I'd kick myself if it turned out badly because I didn't help."

"You're a real peach," Jack said as they pulled up to a red light.

Saturday afternoon was getting ready for the evening. A loud sports car pulled alongside Valerie's sedan, and the occupants ogled the good-looking officer. The driver revved his engine and made suggestive gestures.

"Where are the cops when you need one?" Valerie

asked. The corners of her mouth turned down as the light changed, and the boys pulled away.

Jack was careful to ease away from the intersection. *No use causing more offense to my passenger,* he thought.

As they approached the city center, the tower that had impressed itself on Jack's memory was impressing itself on the eyes of all who drove in from the west. The sun was still above the horizon, and the reflection of the gold-colored windows on Mr. Herties' monument to free enterprise made it stand out more than usual. At least the offensive glare that bothered drivers on summer evenings was absent as winter approached and days shortened.

They drove to the police station, where Jack parked Valerie's car. They walked together to the main entrance. Jack held the door for Valerie, and they ascended the stairs to the reception area.

The attendant recognized Valerie. They both signed in, and the officer immediately buzzed Val and Jack through to the inner offices, where the duty officers in the detective division might be found.

Chapter Ten
Getting Closer

Detective Keegan Willis was sitting at his desk, looking out across the city. He twiddled a pen between his fingers. He did not notice Valerie and Jack when they walked toward him.

"Good afternoon, Keegan," Jack said, trying not to let his distain for the officer show through.

"Ah, Jackie my boy, and Constable Cummins, to what do we owe this little visit?"

"Bruce filled you in, didn't he, about the Herties case?" Jack asked.

The detective swiveled his chair to face his visitors and hoisted his feet to the corner of his desk.

"Well, he said that Old Moneybags was a little miffed that his princess hadn't been in touch for a while. Said it might develop into something, and to keep our ears open for any news."

"Yeah, well it looks like something is developing, and we

may need your help. I mean Herties may need your help. We're just interested citizens at the moment," Jack said.

He wanted to be careful not to appear as if he was trying to do Willis' job. As much as possible, he wanted to be able to use the police resources to advantage. Keegan Willis was always suspicious of Jack's motives.

"Well, let me tell you," Willis said, "I would want to hear from dear old Dad about that. I can't just go flying around the city on some wild goose chase simply on your say-so."

"We're not asking you to do anything of the sort," Valerie said. She felt it in Jack's best interests if he didn't have the opportunity to respond to Willis' remarks.

The detective stiffened visibly but did not change the position of his feet on the desk.

Looking over his shoulder at Jack, he asked, "Then what is it you are wanting with us? Herties' baby is incommunicado. There has been no missing persons report. All you have is some sort of bad feeling in your gut?"

"Where's Ted?" Jack asked.

"He's around here somewhere. He's been reading files all day. Not much goes on, on a Saturday, until later in the evening. Probably things will get more exciting later on. I don't really care. We're off at eight."

Willis reached over his desk for a mug of what appeared to be stale coffee. The powdered creamer had left an oily ring around the perimeter of the dark liquid. Willis sipped, made a face, put the mug down, and pushed it as far away as possible with the tips of his fingers.

He continued, "They say that Herties has been told not to contact us. What's the story there?"

For all his show of disinterest, the detective took his job seriously. He was just less serious when he was dealing with those he considered to be below him in the pecking order or, in Jack's case, social status. Jack's failings in the past were a constant encouragement to Willis, or so it seemed.

Jack and Valerie did their best to explain the situation to the detective, who listened with little sign of emotion. He twiddled his thumbs and looked at his hands as they spoke of their suspicions. Jack carefully edited out some of the more salient points, hoping that Ted Brown, Willis' boss, would show up soon and bring a little more decorum to the room.

Willis had not asked his visitors to sit since they arrived. He seemed uninterested in them or their concerns.

Jack pulled an office chair into the cubicle and placed it for Valerie to use. Then he walked over to Willis' desk, cleared a space, and sat on the edge.

"It is certainly refreshing to see that the police department has not lost its sense of purpose or its desire to serve and protect," Jack said.

Valerie winced visibly.

Willis opened his mouth to speak.

Just then, a door at the far end of the office opened, and the chief detective strode in.

"Hi there, Jack," Ted Brown called across the empty office. "What's new and exciting?" He walked toward Willis' cubicle.

"Well, your sidekick here has been filling us in on the intricacies of the law, in relation to missing persons. We were trying to get a little bit of assurance from your department that, if anything should develop in the Herties situation, we could call on your expertise and your legal powers to bring this to a reasonable conclusion."

"I see no problem with that at all. You understand, though, that without a formal report, there isn't anything we can do."

"That's the way it should be," Jack said. "In fact we are depending on you not to do anything official for the moment. Herties has been told that he is not to contact the police."

"Hold on there, Jack." The chief detective was on full alert now. "This puts a whole new light on things. We were told to be on the lookout for the girl. The chief thought she might have headed off somewhere with friends. Told us to report back when, and if, she came across our path.

"Are you saying that there has been some contact from an individual who claims to have abducted W. D. Herties' daughter?" Brown asked.

Now Willis looked both interested and upset that this last tidbit of information had not been shared earlier.

"I—we—are trying to be as up-front with you as we can, Ted. We have no idea who the guy is. And he hasn't been calling Herties. He's phoned my friend Eric Howes a few times. We probably wouldn't be involved at all if the guy hadn't misdialed the number. He's off by one digit."

"We need to be on this thing right away," Brown said. Keegan nodded emphatically while looking daggers at Jack.

"Here's the deal," Jack said. "Eric has no intention of reporting some crackpot crank caller who says he has Eric's daughter. Eric has no kids. Unless and until this guy calls Herties, you have nothing to pursue.

"I'm asking you guys to sit tight. Herties is in with us, and we have some plans, but if you folks move too early, or the abductor suspects that the girl's father has contacted you, Jennifer's life could be in serious jeopardy."

"That's a very fine line you're walking, Jack, and you know it," Brown said. "I could arrest you for obstruction of justice. I could go to Herties myself and let him know the error of this course of action."

"And you could kiss your job good-bye when W. D. Herties withdraws his financial support of community policing, if this thing goes south," Jack replied.

Brown thought about that. Willis bit his lower lip. Valerie smiled at Jack's little ploy. The sun began to dip below the horizon outside the windows of the detective division of the Metropolitan Police Department.

"My suggestion is that we work together on this," Jack said. "You guys will get the collar when it is all over. For now, I need you to trust me. I have a plan that will fully involve you, eventually. We've just got to take some detours to our final destination. I'll try to make the trip scenic, if you'll work with me."

"All right, Jack," Brown said. "We'll cut you some slack, for the sake of Herties and the girl. Just don't go off trying to handle this all by yourself."

"I'll keep an eye on him, sir. I'll make sure he is careful." Valerie gave the detective a smile.

"I'm glad to hear that, Constable. But I know Jack. Be careful. He can be pretty persuasive. Don't let him get you into something you'll regret later. Don't make me regret letting you two work your plan," the chief detective said.

"Trust me, sir. I'll keep out of trouble," Valerie replied.

"It's Jack I'm more concerned about."

Brown took a swing at Willis' feet and knocked them off the desk.

"Okay, Willis," he said, "back to work. You can help me sort through some of these files. And I'm putting you in charge of making sure that our part of the plan works. You and Jack will work together when we are officially on the case."

Willis' face suddenly sagged as if he had lost all control of his facial muscles. The news of his assignment was obviously not what he had expected.

Jack had a broad smile that betrayed his obvious pleasure at being unofficially placed ahead of the young detective.

"It's okay, Willis. I won't need you for a while yet. You can do the filing, and I'll get back to you later," he said.

Willis had a look that would have cut through metal, if he had been able to harness the heat of his anger.

Jack and Valerie said good-bye, promising to be in touch as soon as things became a little clearer. They left the office and walked down the stairs to the main entrance.

"You enjoyed making Willis feel like the underdog, didn't you?" Valerie asked as they crossed to the parking lot.

"The man gets just a little too full of himself at times. Besides, it wasn't my idea that he be my sort-of second in command."

"I always thought I was your sort-of second in command—sort of," Val said with a pout.

"You are, but I'm not about to tell Detective Willis that. It might hurt his feelings."

Chapter Eleven
Everybody Loves Saturday Night

It was Saturday night. Jack was feeling the pressure of time. There were people to be interviewed, and not a lot of time to track down the person who meant to do harm to Jennifer Herties.

Byron Leach was still a major suspect, especially now that he wasn't where he had been expected to be.

Maybe he had just decided to spend the evening away from home. Maybe he had been at a friend's house, sleeping off a little too much beer. Or maybe he had been off making sure his hostage remained safe and sound. The truth of his whereabouts would have a major influence on what Jack did next.

It would look strange if someone showed up in the evening and started interrogating the kid. Besides, Jack wasn't feeling up to a confrontation at this point. Willis had been enough of a drain on his resources. And besides, he had a good-looking police officer in the seat beside him. If the night had to involve police business, he would prefer something that they could work on together.

Jack started the car and pulled out of the almost deserted parking lot.

"I'm going to drive us to my place. I'll let you drive home. I'm going to get cleaned up, and I'll meet you at your apartment. Chinese all right with you? I'm buying," he said.

"Since you put it that way, how can I resist?"

"I'm afraid I have an ulterior motive," Jack replied.

"Really?" she said with a raise of the eyebrows.

"We're going to be doing some research tonight. I've got to do some preliminary work on the other suspects."

"I'm disappointed." Valerie pretended to pout at the news.

"At least we'll be together. You can help me. Beats doing this all alone. Besides, you get dinner out of it."

The lights in the shops had come on. The streets were ablaze with neon. The sky had turned a dark blue with a tinge of purple at the horizon. It was one of the few cloudless fall nights that the city was likely to experience before the rains of winter came in full force.

Jack drove back to his apartment. Valerie warned him severely about his reckless disregard for the law when he pulled his regular U-turn in front of the building. He apologized. She said she would let him off with a warning and left him standing on the sidewalk.

Jack felt in his pocket for his keys, opened the door to the stairs, and started up to the third floor. He gave only a cursory glance at his office on the way by. No one had kicked the door in, and there were no notes pinned to it. *A good sign,* he thought and continued up another flight.

He got out of his clothes and showered. He checked his answering machine while he toweled off his hair. There were no messages.

He called Eric and learned that, as he had suspected, the mysterious caller was sticking to his one-call maximum. How might that change as the day of the money drop approached, Jack wondered. He told Eric about the visit to Willis and Brown at the police station, and reminded his friend to remain vigilant.

"Remember who you are supposed to be."

"Sir, I'll have you know that you are speaking to W. D. Herties, the richest man in town. I called off the date. You owe me, big time."

"That's the way. Just don't get too cocky. I know the real W. D. I can tell you two apart."

"I met him too. Remember?"

"Look, we're getting closer to the drop," Jack added. "Be careful, and keep track of everything our caller says. You never know what might be important later."

"I'll remember, Jack. Keep in touch."

After he hung up, Jack returned to his plans for the night. He changed into a clean shirt and pants. After running the electric razor over his face and pronouncing himself handsome enough, he splashed on some cologne from a bottle Valerie had given him at Christmas the year before.

"You never know what there might be time for," he said to the image reflected in the bathroom mirror.

He called the little Chinese restaurant that he and Valerie

frequented when they were in an Oriental mood. They had been impressed by the way the vegetables were cooked: not too hard, and not so soft that they became unpalatable. The place was also noted for its large portions, something Jack liked, especially when he had to do an all-nighter. Unfortunately, that was how the evening was shaping up.

Jack locked up and headed downstairs to where his car was parked. He drove to the restaurant to pick up the dinner he had ordered. He was informed it would be a few more minutes.

The owner had got to know Jack from his frequent visits and wanted to talk. They spent a few minutes discussing football. The Asian gentleman still was not too clear on the game, and Jack felt obliged to help with his education.

The topic of weather came up, and they did a comparison between fall in North America and the same season in Asian countries.

A girl with beautiful features and long, straight, jet-black hair came to the front of the restaurant with two paper bags. To the top of one of these was stapled a receipt and a copy of the take-out menu.

The girl made a small bow to the proprietor and then turned to Jack to hand him the parcels. He held up a finger to indicate she should hold them for a moment while he dug his wallet out of his pocket. He looked at the receipt on the bag and counted off some bills. The girl placed the bags on the counter, seeing that the transaction would be too difficult while Jack had the money and she was weighted down with the food.

"Keep the change," he said as he picked up the brown bags.

The girl gave a little curtsy and busied herself with the keys on the cash register.

Jack said good-bye to the proprietor and headed back to the car. The smell of Chinese food heightened his feelings of hunger during the trip to Valerie's apartment complex. He got out of the car, knowing that the odors would still be there when he returned to head home. What tantalized now might nauseate later, once his hunger was sated. He'd find out soon enough, he supposed.

At the door, he responded to Valerie's "Who's there?" with "Delivery guy."

"Come on up, and see me, big fella," was the response.

Jack took the elevator to Valerie's floor. She had changed clothes too. She was wearing a dress that showed off her trim body. Police training had made her firm.

As he unloaded the food on the counter, Jack thought to himself that if the evening had to be occupied mostly with the business at hand, at least it was nice that the scenery would be appealing.

"You've outdone yourself this time, Jack." Valerie peered into the boxes and aluminum containers, and breathed in the steamy odors coming from them.

"It wasn't me. Mr. Lin has taken a liking to me. He always makes sure there is plenty of food. I think there are some extras in there that I didn't even order," Jack said, moving closer and pulling down the edge of a bag to look in.

"Well, it's a lovely selection. Let's get this on some plates and enjoy our dinner before we start the business portion of our meeting. I have some white wine that might go well with this. What say we give it a try?" Valerie asked.

"Well, just a little. I've got to keep my wits about me if I'm going to solve this thing and find the perp."

"Boy, you must have been watching all the wrong programs on TV lately. *Perp* is a term that is hardly ever used by real law enforcement people. Don't get me started on the liberties they take on some of those shows."

"Sorry. I didn't want us to get off on the wrong foot to-night." Jack made a sad face that brought a laugh from his dinner partner.

"Let's eat. You pour the wine," Val said, adding, "I don't have my fine china out tonight. I trust you will forgive me for not putting all this stuff in serving bowls. I'll at least give you a decent plate."

Jack went into the kitchen and opened the wine.

"Interesting brand, this: ROCKHAVEN ESTATES. What's that all about?"

"It's a home brew. I've got a couple of friends who run a bed and breakfast on the West Shore, over in Victoria. They make their own wine and put the name of their little inn on the label. They gave me a couple of bottles to try. I rather like it."

"Good vintage. Bottled in March 2006."

"Hey, you said you wanted to keep your wits about you tonight. It's aged enough for my liking."

For the next hour, they passed the cardboard and aluminum containers back and forth and tried to talk about something other than Jennifer Herties, her father, or the crime someone was in the process of committing against them.

After the meal, Jack helped Valerie clean up. Valerie put on the coffee, and they settled in for a brainstorming session.

"I promise you, I'll make it up to you once this is all over. I know it's a heck of a way to spend a weekend, and I'd like to have you with me tomorrow too," Jack said.

"I'm as concerned as you are, Jack. More so, because it's my job. And you know what they say, 'Two heads are better than one.' "

"As long as you're sure." He patted her hand and looked deeply into her eyes for confirmation.

"I'm sure." She leaned forward and kissed him on the forehead.

"Herties mentioned some of Jen's old friends," Jack said. "He talked about disagreements they had had. I'm not sure some of his reasons for suspecting them are all that valid."

"Jack, it's his daughter. He's anxious to get her back safely. He's certain to overanalyze some of these past relationships—give us false leads. Let's just look at what we have," Val replied.

"Like I said before, I want to check out that old boyfriend who wasn't where he was supposed to be. We'll pay Byron Leach a little visit in the morning. Maybe talk to his folks. I wonder if we can break the silence about her father's concern without tipping our hand about the kidnapping."

Valerie thought a moment. Finally she said, "I think we

might need to be careful a little while longer. If we talk to someone who has Jennifer hidden away and suggest that W. D. has brought us in to investigate, we will be jeopardizing Jennifer. It's just too risky. I think we have to become the aunt and uncle for a little while longer."

"I wonder," Jack said, "did the guy say not to tell anyone, or just not to involve the police? Can't we just be interested friends who are trying to track her down?"

"It sounds really risky to me." Valerie leaned her head on the back of the couch and closed her eyes.

"Let's think about it some more, later," Jack said. "I think we need to call up Mr. Herties and see if we can get some information about the one suspect that he has had personal contact with."

"And who might that be?" She lifted her head and looked at the notepad that Jack had pulled from his pocket.

"His name is, let's see, Fretz. Bernard Fretz was recently fired by Herties. It seems that he was not thrilled to lose his job. Less thrilled with the severance package he was given."

"Could be he wants some more money?" Val asked.

"Maybe. But it sounds kind of far-fetched for someone like that to seek vengeance by kidnapping the boss's daughter." Jack looked at Valerie for affirmation.

"You'd be surprised, some of the excuses I've heard for why people do things. I hear even stranger ones, from guys like Willis and Brown."

"Well, okay then, let's give W. D. a call," Jack said. "You still have your speakerphone? Saves a lot of repeating, and we need to use our time profitably."

"It's right there, already plugged in," Val replied. "Got a long cord that should reach the coffee table."

Jack got up and carried the phone to the table in the middle of the room. He and Valerie moved to the center of the couch so the telephone would pick up both their voices, and so they could hear W. D. Herties.

Jack took out the card with the man's home number on it.

"What a difference one number can make," he commented as he dialed, being careful to insert the corrected digit. He didn't want to get Eric on the line just yet.

Valerie went to check the coffee. The machine had finished its gurgles and burps a few minutes ago, but it always took a little extra time for all the water to get through the filter. The coffee was ready. She gathered cups and picked up the carafe with her free hand.

The phone on the other end of the line could be heard ringing.

"I hope he's home," Jack said as Valerie returned a second time with spoons, cream, and sugar bowl.

"Hello. Herties residence." The voice was clipped. British. A servant of the Herties family.

"Good evening. My name is Jack Elton and I'm . . ."

"Just a moment, sir." The voice showed signs of recognition. "Mr. Herties mentioned that you might call. He said I should pass you straight through. Just a moment, please."

The line went quiet for a moment. There was a click, and the familiar voice of W. D. Herties came through the speaker on the coffee table.

"Jack, what's happening? Do you have any information?"

"Nothing yet, I'm afraid, sir. I have Valerie here with me, and we're hoping to get some things sorted out so we can plan what we should do tomorrow. We're using the speaker phone. Can you hear me all right?" Jack asked.

"Oh, yes. Just fine, Jack. Hi, Valerie."

"Good evening, sir."

"Mr. Herties," Jack continued, "We want to pick your brain about some of the folks you suggested to us, as suspects, for lack of a better word.

"Byron Leach continues to be a person we're interested in. He wasn't home when he was visited this morning, and his parents didn't know where he had gone. What else can you tell us about him?"

Jack leaned back as he waited for Herties' reply. His pen was poised over his notepad.

The millionaire cleared his voice.

"Well, there isn't a whole lot to add to what I've already told you. As I mentioned, Jennifer knew him best. I'd only met him a couple of times. What I know of him is only by reputation, and any opinions I've formed about him are based on what I've heard from Jen and the pain he caused her."

"Persistent, is he?" Valerie wanted to know.

"I'd say so. Wouldn't take 'get lost' for an answer. He was still showing up from time to time, from what I can gather. I guess I suspect him most because I guess I wouldn't put it past him to arrange this so he could have her to himself."

"But what about the demand for money?" Jack asked.

"That is difficult, isn't it?" Herties said. "If he planned to keep her, or thought he could, he probably wouldn't be thinking of asking for money to give her back. I guess you've got me there." There was the sound of resignation in the man's voice.

"We'll check him out some more, in any case. Maybe he has some other motive," Jack said.

"I really appreciate what you are doing," Herties replied.

"You know we've spoken to Jen's cheerleading friend, Margaux," Jack said. "I don't think there's much to worry about there. Barring some new revelation, I think we can strike her off the list. I think that if this all works out the way we want it to, Margaux might want to be Jen's friend again. Of course, that will be up to Jennifer."

Herties did not respond to Jack's comment.

"I've got another name here," Jack said. "Marcus Hardin. What's the connection there?"

"He was another suitor. Jen disliked him from the start, but he kept trying to impress her. I haven't seen him around lately. He was just a name who came to mind."

"Any idea where he might be?" Valerie asked.

"Last I heard, he was working up in the oil fields. He was a big, strong guy. That sort of thing would have suited him. Haven't heard anything else since. He had moved out of his parents' place, so if he's around I'd expect you'd find his number in the phone book."

Valerie went to a drawer, pulled out a telephone directory, and began thumbing through it as Jack continued his conversation.

"Let's look at this one fellow you mentioned who used to work for you. He was fired, wasn't he?"

"You mean Bernard Fretz. Yes, he was fired. Interesting story, that."

"Care to tell me about it?" Jack made a note in his book.

"Fretz worked in accounting. Good man, as far as it went. Came in with a great resume. Impeccable credentials. No problems with him until about three months ago."

"Uh, huh." Jack was jotting the details in his book.

"We started noticing discrepancies between the books and what the bank had on record. It appeared that money was leaking out somewhere."

Jack nodded, forgetting that his hearer could not see the gesture.

Herties continued, "To make a long story short, cash was being siphoned off the top and ending up heaven knows where. The deposits didn't match what the books said the income was. We traced it, naturally enough, to accounting."

"And Fretz was the guilty party?"

"Yes. At least, I think so. We have a pretty tight system of checks and balances down there, being as how we deal with such large amounts of money. We've got someone whose job it is to trace any inconsistencies. We put him on the case, and he came back with Fretz's name."

"Who is this guy?" Jack asked, poised to write the name.

Jack saw Valerie making signs to him out of the corner of his eye. He turned to see that she was pointing at the phone book, and shaking her head.

"Schreiver. That was his name, Ben Schreiver."

"Was?" Jack asked.

"Yes, he quit about a month ago. Left the country, actually. Said he'd had enough of the rainy winters.

Wanted to go to a place that was drier. Hated to see him go, actually. He was a good man."

"Interesting." Jack made another note and showed it to Valerie. She read it and looked up. Both exchanged looks of dismay.

Jack continued, "Oh, sir, Valerie has been scanning the phone directory. It looks like our man Hardin is no longer in the area, as far as they are concerned. We'll check it out further, but we may be able to take him off the list as well."

"What does that leave us with?" Herties asked.

"Well, there's the Leach boy and Bernard Fretz. Margaux may have been lying to us, but I doubt it. The caller is definitely male. I don't know that she is that persuasive, that she could get a boyfriend to pull off a stunt like this."

"I suppose you're right."

"And sir . . ."

"Yes?" Herties asked.

"There's Schreiver."

"You don't really think he's the one who has my Jennifer?"

"I don't know. Did he say where he was going?"

"California, I think. He wanted a warm place, he said."

Valerie shrugged at Jack's inquisitive look and mouthed, "Maybe. Has he come back here lately?"

"You're sure he's moved away. He hasn't come back here at all?" Jack asked.

"I'm pretty sure. He still sends postcards to the office. I saw one just this past week. I think he must still be there."

"Okay, then. That's where we are at the moment.

Valerie and I are going to go over all this tonight and plan our next move. If we need anything else, can I call you in the morning?"

"Feel free. If at all possible, I'd appreciate your holding off till after eight, though. Sundays are my day of rest."

Jack smiled. Valerie covered her mouth to stifle a laugh. Obviously, Herties didn't know what rest was, if sleeping till after eight was his idea of taking it easy.

"I'll be sure to remember that, sir. You have a good evening now," Jack said.

"Thanks, Jack. Talk to you tomorrow. Good night, Valerie."

"Good night, sir," Valerie said.

Valerie pushed the button on the phone, and the line went quiet.

"Looks like we've got ourselves a little intrigue at Herties Enterprises. You think Ben Schreiver was putting his hands in the till and blaming Fretz?" she asked as she refilled Jack's coffee.

"It was my first impression, after hearing Herties' account," Jack said. "I'm not sure he's the kidnapper, though. If he left town with the cash, he'd be pretty foolish to come back and try to extort some more."

"It presents us with some interesting possibilities, that's for sure. Now what?" she asked.

They spent the rest of the evening plotting their moves for the next day.

Another visit to the old boyfriend, Byron Leach, was at the top of the list. If he didn't materialize, it was planned that his parents would be advised of the pressing need to find him. Jack wasn't sure whether he might threaten arrest. It all depended on the response he got.

An intensive check into local records to see if Marcus Hardin was still in the oil fields would be helpful in determining whether he should be considered a suspect.

Bernard Fretz would be worth the visit, if only to get his thoughts on Ben Schreiver's accusations. Jack had decided that that was the best line of attack in the fired employee's case. He would pass himself off as someone investigating the investigator and perhaps learn enough about both men that he and Valerie could decide whether either was worth pursuing as the kidnapper.

The truth was, they had very few leads, and the case had not given up any secrets. Jack knew that without some clue from the abductor, they would be fighting uphill and might not come close to winning the battle.

"Got any brainstorms about how we might move this along a little faster?" he asked Valerie.

"We just keep doing what we've been doing," she said. "You know how boring police work is. We have long periods of plodding detective work and boring documentation, interspersed with brief moments of stark terror and shorter spurts of mind-blowing brilliance. We need to keep digging and listening."

"Are we asking the right questions? Are we talking to the right people?" he asked.

"Jack, we're doing the best we can. Now tomorrow, I'm going to do a little police work to try to get some information that only law enforcement people can get. I intend to either confirm or eliminate the lovesick football player as a suspect. That'll be one down."

"How soon can you do that?" Jack asked.

"I can use the office computer to do some searching in the local records. If the guy has come back to town and been here any length of time, there will be some record of that—real estate sales, lease registrations, auto licensing—that sort of thing.

"Before I go to bed tonight, I can call my friends up in Fort McMurray and ask them if they can track down our man Marcus in the oil field. If he's there, the whole process will be a lot easier."

"Am I glad I've got you on my side. You are truly a force to be reckoned with," Jack said, obviously awestruck.

"Aw, you're just saying that so I won't cite you for your infamous U-turns."

"You've got me, Officer. I surrender." Jack winked at his partner.

"Well, don't surrender just yet. There's work to be done."

Jack made notes in his book as Valerie spoke. He underlined names and details that he thought particularly important, and numbered the steps they planned to take.

"Okay, you've got Hardin pretty much covered," he said finally. "I'll pick you up in the morning. You can let me know then if we have to chase after him. We'll visit the Leach family and try to question Byron. I don't know about Fretz. I guess I'll call Herties and get the last known address, as we say in the police biz. What happens next will depend on where he is, and what we know, by that time. I still think we'll go with the 'investigator' line, and see how sympathetic he is. He might give us a lead on Schreiver that will take us in that direction."

Jack placed an emphatic double underline beneath Ben Schreiver's name. He looked toward Valerie, who had begun to clear away the coffee and cups.

"I guess I'd better be going, as soon as we've cleared up. Tomorrow will be a pretty busy day," he said.

"I'm kind of hoping it will be a turning point in this whole thing. Otherwise, you'll be on your own," Valerie replied. "I'll have to give up the amateur sleuthing and return to my day job of professional sleuthing on Monday morning."

Jack laughed. "Sounds pretty boring, if you ask me."

"Yeah, but the pay's better."

"If this ever turns into a regular job, I'll start charging for my services. So far folks have been sufficiently thankful that they give me something for my efforts. If worse comes to worst, I can write my memoirs and live off the royalties."

"Let me know. I'll buy a copy," Valerie said.

Jack helped with the last of the clean-up and said good night to Valerie. They shared a lingering embrace at the apartment door, and he headed for the elevator.

"Don't forget to call your friends in Alberta," he called over his shoulder as he walked down the hall.

"I'll get on it right away," she said. "It will take them a while to do a check. Talk to you in the morning."

With that, Valerie went back into her apartment and closed the door.

Jack rode down to the lobby and walked to the car. As he had suspected, the odors of Chinese food greeted him on the air that wafted out of the open car door. Cold, the smells weren't nearly as appetizing as they had been in the apartment.

He felt a creeping loneliness as he drove home. On sidewalks and through café windows, he could see couples enjoying the final hours of their night out together. He regretted that his night out had been mostly for the benefit of others. Then he chastised himself for his selfishness.

The time would come when the pressures of other people's business would not weigh so heavily on him. Then it would be Jack and Valerie who were sitting and laughing and drinking in the warmth of a bar, or walking arm-in-arm along the street.

He had been a bachelor for so long that it seemed the natural thing. But he felt the same emptiness every time he returned to his dim little apartment. He wondered whether these thoughts that were flooding his brain were only motivated by a desire for convenience, or whether there was something else.

He thought about Valerie. All he could think about was Valerie. There had been other girls in the past, but they didn't have the same effect on him that she had. He knew some of their names but could not conjure up a single image.

Valerie, on the other hand, popped into his mind fully fleshed out and complete, down to the finest detail. Could she be the one true love he had been seeking all this time? It would be fun to take the idea for a spin sometime. Of course, that was not likely to happen. Valerie came from the sort of family where living together before the wedding just was not done, no matter what was becoming the norm.

He reflected on his own mother's question, whenever he had protested that everyone else was doing one thing or another, "Would you jump off the railway bridge into the river just because all your friends did?"

He couldn't help smiling as he drove. His mother always expected and received a negative reply. If he had been honest, the answer would have been, "Not again."

No, he cared about this beautiful peace officer. He respected her for who she was and for the work she did. He was not about to jeopardize that relationship. The more he thought about it, though, the more the thought of marriage and a lifetime of bliss with that same woman appealed to him.

He pulled up to his building, and the thought appealed to him more. He was amazed at how thinking about her made the minutes, and the miles, fly by.

Up in his apartment again, Jack went through the nightly ritual that would bring him eventually to his bed. Tonight it was unmade. The rush to get ready for the day that was just ending had not allowed for him to perform those sorts of tasks.

He sat on the edge of the bed and turned the TV to the news channel. "Nothing much new," he said to himself. "The same people killing the same people, and getting killed in return. Governments doing what governments do, and getting no respect, sometimes because they don't deserve it."

The local report included a story about some teenagers who had got themselves drunk and then tried to race on the Trans-Canada Highway. Their race had ended with their lives against the concrete abutment of an overpass. Close as they were to the hospital, there had been nothing the paramedics could do for them.

"Wasted youth," Jack muttered and turned off the light.

Chapter Twelve
Just the Facts

Sunday morning dawned bright and fair. As Jack looked out on the road in front of his apartment, he could see that it was going to be another of those rare fall days in the city when there would be no rain. Now if only the sun would shine brightly on the investigation that would shortly be at hand, all would truly be well with the world.

It was before eight, and Jack dared not bother W. D. Herties for directions before the time appointed by the dear man, who considered it a day of rest if he did not rise until 8:30. He hoped that Valerie had been successful with her inquiries to the police in northern Alberta. He prayed that Marcus Hardin had learned the value of hard work and was devoting himself to digging in the dirt for black gold.

Jack dressed and put a fresh charge of grounds in the coffee maker. While it brewed, he reviewed the notes from the night before and added a few reminders to himself about the sorts of things he needed to know.

His phone rang a little after eight.

"Time to get up, sleepyhead," Valerie's cheerful voice came through the receiver.

"I am up. Have been for some time now. Who's the sleepyhead then?"

"I've been working. I have some good news and some bad news for you."

"Shoot," Jack said.

"Okay, here is the info on Hardin. Good news is he is still up north. As far as we can figure out, he has been there for some time. No time off. No time away. We can scratch him off the suspect list."

"What's the bad news?"

"I've been called in to do a death call. You hear about that accident over by the hospital last night?"

"Yeah, what about it?" Jack asked.

"One of the kids was so badly mangled that they didn't identify him till about an hour ago. Kid lived with his mom. Dad's been absent for a while. They want me to go with one of our guys to offer some comfort when he breaks the news.

"I'm going to be tied up for a little while. Choice is yours. You can wait for me, or you can go ahead to the Leach place. You can pick me up afterward, and we'll go to wherever the accountant, Fretz, is living."

Jack's face and heart both fell at the news. These things happen, he supposed, but why now, when they needed to be chasing after the answers to so many questions?

"I still need to call Mr. Herties and get an address for Fretz. Then I had better check in with Eric and see if he's heard anything," Jack said.

"I'll call your place once I'm finished and see if you're back," Valerie said.

"Here's a better idea. I've got my cell phone with me. I'll call you as soon as I'm clear of all this."

"Unless you want to show up with a uniformed police officer, I'll have to come back here to change. Let's play it by ear."

"I'll have my ear ready and waiting," Jack said.

Jack waited until almost nine before dialing Herties' number. The phone on the other end was answered on the first ring.

"I was starting to think you weren't going to call," the millionaire said.

"No fear of that, sir. I just wanted to be sure that I wasn't disturbing your rest."

"When it comes to family, there's nothing you might do that would bother me, except, of course, do nothing," came the reply.

"I'll remember that, sir. Now, I wonder if you could track down some information for me."

Jack asked Herties for Fretz's address. The information was soon retrieved, and Jack looked on a map to see where he was located. It appeared that the former accountant for Herties Enterprises was living in the suburbs to the north-west. It would be easy to do the rounds of questioning. The two families lived within a few minutes of each other.

Jack called Eric as soon as he was off the phone with Herties. The line was busy.

Best to wait a few minutes before I head out, Jack thought to himself.

His phone rang.

"I've been trying to contact you, Jack. Your line has been busy. I got another call from the guy." Eric sounded panicky.

"What did he say?" Jack asked.

"He reminded me that I'd better have the cash by tomorrow, or the girl would be in trouble. Say, Jack, Herties will have the money, won't he?"

"I think he's got enough money to buy back his daughter many times over," Jack said.

"Yeah. But, this guy wants cash. We gotta have a briefcase full of real money for this guy."

"Don't worry. It's taken care of. Now, what else did he say?"

"He said I should be by the pay phone at the minimall to the west of here at ten in the morning tomorrow. No police. He'll be watching. I'll get more instructions then."

"Anything else you can remember that might help us figure out who this guy is?"

"Nothing I can think of. I must say, though, he sounds kind of full of his own importance."

"How so?" Jack asked.

"He keeps saying how sly he is."

"In so many words?"

"No, not quite, he keeps saying . . . Let me think. He keeps saying he's 'sly as a fox, if you know what I mean.' "

"He uses that phrase, 'if you know what I mean'?" Jack asked, intrigued.

"Yeah. Interesting, isn't it? And I have no idea what he means."

"Me neither. Probably an affectation of sorts, like people who say 'ya know' after every statement they make."

"Probably. That's all I have, Jack. Sorry I can't be more helpful."

"If you think of anything else, let me know. I'll be running around all day. If you can't get through right away, it's because my phone is off and I'm in the middle of an interrogation, I mean interview."

Jack chuckled at the reference.

The two men agreed to be in touch throughout the day. Jack suggested that Eric try to tape the caller the next time he phoned.

"Open up the lid of your answering machine, Eric. Is there a button in there that says 'record'?"

"Yeah, I think so."

"Give it a push, and tell me what happens."

"Okay, the tape is rolling. Now what?"

Jack slipped into his coat as he talked, moving the phone from one hand to the other as he ran each arm into the sleeves.

"Just keep talking for a little bit then press STOP, or PAUSE, or whatever button you use for your message tape."

"It's stopped," Eric said.

"Rewind it, and hit PLAY."

Jack could hear the sound of the tape whizzing and then the *snap* when it came to the end. There was a click, as Eric pushed the Play button. Now Jack could hear the last few sentences of their conversation coming from the speaker of Eric's answering machine.

"That sounds like it will work. Have you got some spare tapes?" Jack asked.

"I've got some the same size that I use in my hand-held recorder. Will they do?"

"They should work fine and may run longer than your message tape. Run and get one and replace it while I'm on the phone. That way, you won't get caught in the middle of a tape change if our guy is trying to call you back."

There was a lengthy pause while Eric went to wherever the spare tapes were stored. Then Jack heard the sounds of his friend fumbling with the answering machine.

"There, it's in. It's a two-hour tape," Eric said finally.

"That should help. Best to keep a spare handy, though. And remember some of these machines operate at a nonstandard speed. You may have less recording time than is indicated on the tape. Keep an eye on it. We want to try to catch every word. Maybe someone will recognize the voice."

Their immediate business concluded, the men hung up. Jack gathered his notes and the address that Herties had provided for Bernard Fretz. He headed down to the front door.

The air was cool as he got into his car. He was thankful for the respite from the rain. It would make the difficult work ahead a little easier to handle.

When he was sure no one was coming, Jack fired up the engine and made a U-turn that headed him toward the west. He thought of Valerie and hoped that her sad duties of the morning would soon be over.

Time to see if Byron Leach was home.

Jack drove right to the Leach residence. It was a little after ten when he arrived.

The house looked to have been built within the past six years or so. It was located in an area where each home appeared to have its own personality. This was a little higher class than some homes, but not quite as lavish as the ones owned by the executives and business owners.

It was faced with stone and had a two-car garage. An older car sat before one of the roll-up doors. It looked a little out of place amidst the signs of affluence.

Jack walked to the door and rang the bell. He could hear a digital tune being played to announce his presence.

Before long, a short, round lady with gray hair bustled to the entrance and opened the door wide.

"Good morning. May I help you?" she asked.

"Mrs. Leach?" Jack asked.

"Yes, I am. And who might you be?" She sounded quite cheery.

Jack introduced himself as a friend of the Herties family.

"We've been a little worried lately about Jen. I understand that my friend Eric was here yesterday. We are terribly anxious to speak to Byron. We know that he was a friend of Jen's and were hoping he might have some idea of where she might be."

"Who's at the door, Mom?" The voice came from somewhere behind the woman.

"It's someone to see you," she called over her shoulder.

Jack heard the sound of bare feet on a wooden floor. Each step also made the floor thunder. It was the sound of an approaching football player.

The hulk in the hallway wore a sleeveless T-shirt with a familiar swoosh graphic on the front. He wore beige training shorts, no socks, and no shoes. What had once been a white baseball cap was perched on the boy's head with the bill around the back and hanging close to his tree trunk of a neck. In one hand he held a cereal bowl. A spoon was between the fingers of the other hand.

"Hi, I'm Jack."

The athlete put the spoon in the bowl, wiped the now-free hand on his shorts, and thrust it out in front of Jack.

"Byron. You wanted to talk to me?"

"Yes. All right if I come in?" Jack asked.

Mom stood back from the door and gestured for the visitor to enter.

Jack was ushered into a spacious den in the middle of the first floor. A large couch dominated the decor. Easy chairs offered other accommodation. A coffee table sat in front of the couch.

Mrs. Leach headed off to do other things, leaving the two men alone.

"Sit wherever you'd like," Byron said.

Jack took a place on the sofa.

"What's this all about?" he asked, lowering his bulk into one of the chairs.

"I'm trying to find out where Jennifer Herties might be. Her dad's a friend of mine and knew I was in the area on business today. Asked if I could drop around and see if you could help. You're a friend of hers, I understand."

"You a cop or something?" the boy asked.

"Oh, no. Nothing like that." Jack tried to remain calm. "Why do you ask?"

"Dunno. It just seems strange for family friends to show up two days in a row, looking for Jen. She in some sort of trouble?"

"I don't think so. So she *is* a friend of yours?" Jack asked again.

Byron shifted in his chair and looked away from Jack. He crossed his arms absentmindedly, then uncrossed them and looked directly at his visitor.

"I guess it depends on your point of view, not that it matters much. I want to be a friend of Jen's, but she doesn't want much to do with me."

"I see." Jack already knew the details but needed to let the boy explain himself. He listened carefully for any hint that Byron wanted to get back at the girl who had dumped him.

Byron explained how the two had gone out together for some time. He had felt that the arrangement was exclusive.

"Jennifer agreed to that for a while but then began dating other guys. When I asked what had made the difference, she accused me of being too possessive and demanding." He had a genuine look of regret on his face.

He admitted to Jack that he had the tendency to overreact to things he perceived as personal slights. He had probably been a little bit angry with his former girlfriend.

"How are things between you now?" Jack asked.

"She still doesn't want to see me—not alone, at least. We share some of the same friends. But we're not, you know, close anymore."

"Seems to me you're better off without her, if that's the way she treated you." Jack watched his reaction.

Byron fixed his eyes on Jack again. His gaze was unflinching.

"No. I think that's unfair. Jen's a nice girl. If I hadn't met someone else, I'd probably still be trying to get back with her."

"You have any idea where I might get hold of her?" Jack asked, still watching closely.

The young man stared off into a corner of the room and tapped his chin with an index finger. He shook his head and turned his attention back to Jack.

"If you can't get her at the college, and her folks haven't seen her at home, I wouldn't know where she could be.

"There was a trip of some sort last weekend," Byron continued. "I wouldn't know if she went on it, but they should have all been back by last Sunday night. That's a week ago today. Gosh yeah, she'd have been back for days."

It appeared that Byron Leach had begun to get over his former girlfriend. Apart from wanting to keep her as a friend, it didn't seem to Jack that the man's interest was a cause for further concern.

"Well, thanks a lot for agreeing to see me. If you hear from Jen, please give her dad a call. You do have his number, don't you?"

"Yeah, I've got one of his cards lying around somewhere. I hope you hear from her soon. I'll check around."

"Thanks. I appreciate it," Jack said.

He was escorted to the door. The two men shook hands. Jack massaged his compressed hand as he walked to the car. The kid had a grip like a vise.

Jack got into his car and looked at his notes. He put a check next to the entry for Byron Leach and pulled out his cell phone. So far, there had been no calls from Valerie. He dialed Eric.

"Herties."

"Good. Keep that up. Any news?" he asked.

"Nothing new. Do I have to sit around here all day?" Eric sounded tired.

"Might be best. You never know when our guy might call. If I stir up some dirt with someone, they might want to be sure that W. D. knows that they don't want cops at the pickup. No one said he couldn't have friends check into the whereabouts of his daughter."

"You're sure this interview stuff is wise?" Eric asked.

"Darned if I know. But I'd like to think that this guy, if he's desperate for the money, won't want to tip his hand by making a threat right after my visit. The cops would be able to nail him.

"I'm going to be heading over to see the guy named Fretz," Jack continued. "He's the one Herties fired. I want to ask him about a Ben Schreiver. You might not have heard about him."

"Don't think you mentioned the name," Eric said.

"He got Fretz fired. He might have been the one skimming some of the boss's cash and blaming it on the accountant. I want to see what Fretz knows about him."

"Valerie with you?"

"Nope. Haven't heard from her since earlier this morning. I'm working alone till she gets back from her police business."

Jack couldn't remember whether he had told Eric about what Valerie was doing and didn't want to get into a long explanation, in case she was trying to call.

"Well, take care, Jack. I'll be monitoring the lines."

"That's good. I'll be in touch."

Chapter Thirteen
The Fool on the Hill

Jack compared the address he'd been given to the map of the city. He had to drive only ten minutes to find Fretz's house.

The former Herties accountant lived in a newer part of town. His home was built on the side of a mountain that dominated the southwest corner of the municipality. The street was a close; it had a dead end with a circular road around which other homes were located. Jack had driven up the long hill to find himself in the loop that would take him back down if he missed the address. He located the Fretz house on the first try. He parked by the sidewalk in front.

The house was built facing up the mountain so that the back of the building was longer than the front. The house was a wedge that fit up against the incline. The main floor was the top, the only one visible from the road.

Jack walked up the path to the front door and knocked.

He could see through the window that there were stairs leading down to a lower level. A large living room was straight ahead. He could see windows looking out onto the back of the property. There did not seem to be anyone around.

Jack pressed a doorbell that had until then escaped his notice. A two-tone chime sounded. He waited to see if there would be any answer. He was about to walk away when he saw someone coming up the stairs from the lower level.

He was a man of middle age, with thinning hair and glasses. He was wearing Levi's and a navy T-shirt. He was wiping his hands on a rag as he walked.

Jack smiled as the door was opened.

"Yeah. Waddaya want?"

Obviously not expecting or wanting anyone, Jack thought. He put out his right hand.

"Hi, I'm Jack. I'm working for Herties Enterprises. Can I ask you some questions about your employment there?"

The man started to close the door.

"I don't work there anymore," the man said. "You wouldn't want my opinion of the place."

"Oh, I think I would. I'm trying to track down a Ben Schreiver. I believe you might be able to help me," Jack said.

The door stopped closing.

"As long as you don't expect me to give that scumbag a good reference, I suppose I could give you a moment of my time. You'll have to make it snappy. I've got stuff to do."

"I'll be as brief as I can. May I come in?" Jack asked.

"Oh, sure," the man said absentmindedly. He opened the door wider and let Jack into the entryway.

"I'm assuming that you *are* Bernard Fretz who used to work in accounting."

"That's me. Schreiver did me in a while back. Accused me of skimming money out of the Herties accounts."

"And were you?" Jack asked.

"Of course not. And here I was, thinking we were going to have a nice, reasonable conversation. You keep asking dumb questions, and we'll be done real quick."

"I'm sorry. I had to ask," Jack said. Fretz's answer was confirming what he had suspected. That was, of course, if the man was being truthful.

"Let me ask you," Jack continued, "do you think this guy Schreiver might have had something to do with the disappearing money?"

Fretz motioned for Jack to move into the living room and offered him a seat.

"I'm almost positive that he had something to do with it. I don't exactly know how, but all of a sudden he had a lot more cash to spend than he had ever had before. Mind you, Herties paid well. We were never lacking for money to live well. But Ben was buying a lot of stuff—cars, jewelry, fancy clothes . . ."

"Where is he now?"

"If he knows what's good for him, he's still down in California, or wherever it was he went to. He comes back here, and he's likely to hear from me."

"How did his actions affect your relationship with the company?" Jack asked.

"Well, first off, W. D. noticed the money was missing.

It was easy to see that it wasn't a simple accounting error. Next he comes to me and asks what I know about it. He shows me the records he has and the bank statements. I could see that something was wrong and told him so. Told him it wasn't my work either. Looked like a separate set of accounts. Next thing I know, Schreiver has been pulled to work on the case. He never asked me any questions. Never spoke to anyone else, as far as I can tell."

Jack could see that the man was becoming agitated. Fretz had stood up and was pacing back and forth as he spoke. His voice rose as he continued his complaint.

"What happened next?" Jack asked.

"Next thing I knew, I was being told my services were no longer needed by the company. They took my keys. They emptied my desk. And a security officer escorted me out of the building.

"Now, I'm waiting for the other shoe to drop," Fretz continued. "Herties hasn't decided how he'll proceed. I'm expecting a court case of some sort. I'd like to do what Ben did and just run away. But you gotta have money for that. Maybe I'll be able . . ."

His voice trailed off, and Fretz's eyes darted back and forth as if he was afraid he had said too much.

"How do you feel about Herties?" Jack asked.

Fretz looked everywhere but at his interrogator. He folded his arms across his chest and leaned against the mantle of the gas fireplace.

"How would you feel?" he asked, a look of disgust on his face.

"I'd probably be pretty angry. I'd probably want to set things right," Jack replied.

"Yeah, well, I thought Herties was pretty quick to let the blame fall on me, as if I hadn't given him the best service I could. There he was, living on the top floor of his glass tower while we collected his money for him. I'd been faithfully serving all those years, and suddenly I'm on the street and out of a job."

He opened his arms to embrace the room.

"Unless I get some money soon," he continued, "I'll have to give up living around here. As it is, this place is sold. Found a buyer about four weeks ago. They move in on Friday. Then I'm out of here."

"Where will you go?" Jack asked.

A shadow passed across the face of Bernard Fretz. The arms folded across his chest again.

"Well, I thought that maybe I'd like to take a little trip south. I've always wanted to see one of those little Caribbean islands where life is slow and nobody knows anybody. Kind of like to catch my breath, so to speak."

"Sounds expensive," Jack offered.

Fretz did not respond.

"Mr. Herties is experiencing a little personal problem these days. A family thing," Jack continued.

Jack watched carefully. Fretz seemed unmoved. By now, he had turned away from Jack and was looking at a painting over the fireplace.

"That's too bad. He's got money." He turned to face Jack before continuing, "I'm sure he will find a way to solve whatever the problem is. It's worked for him before."

Jack was making careful mental notes at this point.

"I guess that's true," Jack conceded. "A lot of things money can buy. Then again, there's a lot it can't."

"Not as far as W. D. is concerned," Fretz said.

"It's his daughter. Some sort of problem. I think they had some kind of argument. She ran away or something."

"That a fact," Fretz said, arms crossed.

"You ever met his daughter?" Jack asked.

"I think I saw Jen once, a long time ago. Good-looking girl, as I remember. I'm not certain I would recognize her now, though."

"She's been studying out here at the college. She might be around town. You're sure you wouldn't recognize her?" Jack asked.

"Pretty sure. But I can always keep an eye out for her. I've got one of Herties' business cards. I can get in touch if I see the girl."

"That would be a great help, I'm sure. I'm glad to hear that you're not holding any of this against him personally," Jack said, unsure of the truth what he was suggesting.

"Well, look," Fretz said. "I've got to get some stuff together so I can be ready for the move. It's been nice talking. I really hope you track down Schreiver. I'll show you to the door."

Jack pulled himself to his feet and headed for the entryway.

"Thanks for your help. I think I've got some of the answers I was looking for. Good luck with your plans."

Jack put out his hand to shake, and Fretz took it. Jack couldn't help but notice that the offered hand was damp and cool to the touch.

"Yeah, I'll be talking to you," Fretz said as he opened the door.

Jack thought that might be a distinct possibility. He got in his car and drove down the hill.

His cell phone rang as he turned the corner, onto the main road back to town.

"Hi Jack. It's Valerie. I'm sorry I didn't get in touch earlier."

"I've just finished talking to Fretz," Jack said. "I think we've got some new evidence. I guess I should say we have our only evidence relating to the case. I think that we may have found our abductor. I'm just not sure how or if we'll be able to do anything before the drop. I'm hoping that our guy makes a mistake."

"So, what are you going to do now?" Valerie asked.

"Not sure. I was hoping that Eric might have something new, but maybe our guy has been tied up for the last little while." Jack wasn't sure that Valerie would catch the point of his last comment.

"You think Fretz is our man?" Valerie asked. "I've only got tonight to be of any help with the private investigation. I'm back to work tomorrow morning. Why don't you come over and we can run through what you've got. That death call was a little more than I expected. I hope I don't have to do that ever again," she added.

Jack could sense the sadness in her voice.

He knew from personal experience that it would happen again, many times. It would never be easy to tell a parent that their son or daughter had died.

"I'm sorry it was so tough," he said. "Listen. I can be there in about half an hour. How about I pick up dinner?"

"I've got a better idea," Valerie said. "I'll cook. You pick up dessert on the way. I'll be waiting to hear about your day. If you are driving while you talk, hang up. And use both hands."

"But you called me," Jack replied.

"And you are supposed to pull over and stop. It's not the law . . . yet. But it's safer."

"Gotta go, then. See ya soon." He snapped the phone shut, felt for the well in the console, and dropped it in.

Chapter Fourteen
Down to the Wire

A few moments later, Jack pulled into the parking lot of a warehouse-style supermarket. It was one of those places that had just about everything. It looked more like a department store than a food purveyor. But it had a bakery, and he needed to buy dessert for his time with Valerie. He selected a cheesecake from the cooler and proceeded to the cash register.

Standing in line, he marveled at the kinds of garbage that passed for news. Tabloids in the area around the check-out proclaimed that Jesus had come back and was living in California. A famous TV star was having a weight problem and had gone over the three-hundred-pound mark, pictures inside. And aliens. Lots and lots of aliens. They were coming from everywhere and doing all sorts of inconvenient things. Read all about it.

Oh, well, he thought. *At least you can approach the cashier with a smile on your face.*

He did just that and headed back to the parking lot.

Jack spent the trip back to the city reviewing the information that he had gleaned from his interview with Bernard Fretz.

The man had been obviously evasive. Though the interrogation had been brief, Jack was convinced that the former accountant knew more than he was letting on.

Was he married? Jack didn't know.

Did anyone else live in the house? Jack hadn't been able to tell. He thought of how convenient it would be to hide someone on the lower floor. There were no windows visible from the road. It might require another visit, perhaps while Fretz was away. *How do you do that?* he asked himself.

He looked at his watch. It was almost four. He had time for a brief stop before going to Valerie's. He pulled off the highway and stopped by the side of the road. He fished out his cell phone and dialed her number.

"Hi Val, it's me. I'm making a detour."

"Where will you be, in case I need you desperately?" she asked.

"I want to go and see Eric. He deserves a face-to-face, after his day at home with the telephone. I'll fill him in and then get over to your place. We're having a cheesecake."

"Yum. I can hardly wait," came her happy response.

"And I'm stopped. Just thought you should know that I do take your advice from time to time."

"Good boy. Keep an eye on the clock. Call me if you're going to be late."

Jack hung up and drove to his friend's apartment

complex. He parked in his usual place and went around to the main entrance, where his friend buzzed him in.

Seated in Eric's living room, Jack filled him in about the day's experiences.

"I'm suspicious of Fretz," he said. "He seems to have a motive. He had the opportunity to grab the girl last week. He's only ten minutes from the college. How he might have done it is the mystery. One of her friends says she left a party, in a pub, after a mysterious phone call. Could have been him. And he's got a place where he might be able to stash someone, for a while, at least."

"What about Byron Leach?" Eric asked.

"I'm pretty certain he had nothing to do with it. I think he just didn't tell his mother he was going out with the boys the night before, and then broke training. Wouldn't want to be seen on the streets in a less-than-sober condition. That's why you didn't find him at home, I suspect."

Jack was telling Eric about Ben Schreiver and his suspected deception when the phone rang.

Eric picked up the receiver, and Jack listened to one side of the conversation.

"Herties here." Eric listened, and then made frantic signs to his friend that it was the mystery caller.

"No. Listen. I can assure you that I have not got the police involved," Eric said into the receiver.

A pause to listen, then, "Well, yes. They are aware that my daughter is missing, but I have not mentioned the contact I have had with you. They think she has run away. They're checking the streets."

Jack gave Eric the thumbs-up. "Ask him if Jen is still okay," he whispered.

Eric asked, listened, and nodded affirmation to Jack.

"What do you want me to do?" Eric asked. Then, "How do I know she will be safe?"

He listened for the answer.

"I see. So, tomorrow morning this will all be over, and I'll have my daughter back." He paused, then, "Very well, then. I'll be waiting to hear from you. Yes, the money will be ready. Good-bye."

He hung up.

"What's going on?" Jack asked.

"He sounded plenty ticked with Herties. Said he'd been watching the neighborhood and knew that someone was asking around. Accused me, er, I mean Herties, of involving the cops.

"He seemed convinced when I assured him that I had not told them about his calls. I figured it was safe to tell him that they know that Jennifer is missing."

"Well, isn't that interesting," Jack said. "He knows that we've been checking around. The only way he could know that is if he's one of the ones we've been talking to.

"I'm no cop, at least not anymore," Jack added. "None of the folks we talked to know me as anything other than who I said I was. Did he say anything else that might confirm his identity?"

"Nothing, Jack. Same old stuff all the time. And it's funny, he introduces himself the same way every time."

"How's that?" Jack asked.

"Your foxy friend," Eric answered.

"What?" Jack leaned forward and cupped his hand to an ear.

"He starts every conversation with 'Hello, this is your foxy friend,' and then he sort of snickers."

"Weird," Jack said. "He sounds as if he's too full of himself for his own good. But Fretz didn't give the impression of being overconfident about his abilities. He just sounded angry. This guy's voice; what's it sound like?"

"I think he's disguising it. It sounds like he's forcing it a bit. I don't think there's anything there that will help."

"Any other sounds on the line that we might be able to identify?" Jack asked.

"No. Actually, I have been paying close attention. It's very quiet, wherever he is."

"Well, not really a lot to go on. I'm still throwing my vote in Fretz's favor."

"He seems to feel that Herties is doing, or has done, something underhanded," Eric said.

"Why do you say that?" Jack asked.

"He's accused me—him—more than once of being a wolf in sheep's clothing."

"Really?" Jack was intrigued now. "And he's used those exact words? The guy obviously has issues. I hope we can nail him. Without being able to get the cops involved just yet, we've got to play it cool, in order to help the girl."

"A miracle wouldn't hurt about now," Eric offered.

Jack agreed.

"Tomorrow is when it all comes down to the wire," Eric said. "He said to expect a call around ten. There will be instructions about where to go to drop off the money."

"I'll get Herties over here with the money, and we'll be ready for the drop, if necessary," Jack said. "Didn't he say something about the pay phone over by the minimall?"

"Yeah, he said he's changed his mind and that I should wait at home for the call."

"Okay, unless you hear something else, I'll be here in the morning with Herties and more money than either of us is likely to see in a lifetime. We'll play it by ear from there."

Jack left his friend and continued the drive to Valerie's.

The early evening traffic was relatively light, and he was able to make the trip in good time. Within an hour or so, the roads would be clogged, as those who had gone elsewhere for the weekend fought their way back into the city and suburbs in preparation for the equally crowded commute the next morning.

Jack was able to find a parking spot close to Valerie's apartment building and was soon in the elevator to her floor. She was waiting for him when he stepped out into the hallway.

He had forgotten the cheesecake in the trunk of the car and had to go back down to get it.

"Hang on. I'll get my coat and come with you," Valerie said.

Jack escorted her to her apartment and waited while she put on a jacket. They rode down in the elevator and walked arm-in-arm to the car, where Jack opened the trunk and extracted the box.

"Gee, it's a big one. We'll never eat it all."

"That's okay," he said as he shifted the container. "It

just means I'll have to come back for a second helping after all this mess is over. Hopefully tomorrow."

When they had finally returned to the apartment, Valerie began the meal preparations.

"So, Jack, where are we, in the information-gathering business?" She stirred a steaming pot of spaghetti and turned down the heat as bubbles began to rise to the rim.

Jack went over the day's events for her and shared his suspicions about Fretz.

"Problem is, we can't get the guy without probable cause, as you folks say. He's ticked with his former employer. He's moving because he can't afford to live in his present location. Says he's taking a vacation. But I think if he gets the cash from Herties, he won't come back."

"You can't do anything, but I can," Valerie said. All we need is the go-ahead from Herties, and the police can get a warrant and search his place for evidence."

"You know he isn't going to do that until he's positive the girl is okay," Jack said. "And that won't happen until after he sees her with his own two eyes. We've only got a few hours before I have to ferry Mr. Herties out to the suburbs for the exchange. He's got to be the one at the phone this time. Our man will be watching. And if there's any sign of you and your colleagues, we may spoil the whole thing."

"Leave it to me," Valerie said. "I'm getting an idea. You'll have to wait until the exchange is about to take place, but maybe we can get this guy before he leaves town."

"Well, I don't have what I need to get this guy before the trade. We've been put in a tough position. I would have liked to give Herties some good news today," Jack said, regret in his voice.

"You may still be able to be the bearer of glad tidings. You'll just have to wait until he's spent his million to retrieve Jennifer. It's pocket change for a guy like him."

"Sure, but I don't want this guy to think he can get away with it, just because his victim can afford the price," Jack said.

"Leave it to me. Now let's eat," Valerie said, heading toward the steaming pot on the stove.

The couple spent the next little while putting the meal together. They talked about everything except W. D. Herties and his missing daughter.

Valerie had prepared a spaghetti dish that Jack was particularly fond of. Garlic bread was warming in the oven. The meal began with a particularly tasty salad. Jack opened a bottle of wine to go with the meal.

After the meal, they relaxed with coffee and enjoyed large servings of the cheesecake Jack had bought.

"Whoa! I don't think I could eat another bite," Valerie said in a pained voice after the last forkful of dessert. "I'm almost afraid to try to put my uniform on in the morning. You're going to have to stop doing this to me, Jack." Her smile betrayed a lack of conviction about the situation.

With dinner over and the dishes in the washer, they sat in Valerie's living room. The wine had had its effect on Jack. The conversation turned again to matters at hand.

"I'm afraid we haven't done enough to try to solve this thing," Jack said.

"What else could have been done?" Valerie asked.

"I'm not sure. It seems to me we could have involved our friends from the police department a little more."

"They'll get their chance," Valerie said. "Besides, I'm a cop too. It's just not an official police case yet."

"I suppose, but I've been frustrated by how slowly things have been moving," Jack said.

"Well, talk to your suspect. He's the one who's been keeping all the secrets to himself," Valerie suggested.

Jack took a sip of his coffee and contemplated a corner of the ceiling. The ideas just weren't coming. He'd have to wait for the morning and see what would happen.

"Mind if I turn on your TV?" he asked.

"Go ahead. Not much on these days. Believe me, I've looked."

Jack picked up the remote from a side table and pressed the button. The television screen brightened, and a home renovation show was in progress.

Jack pressed some buttons, and now a local news program appeared. A young Asian woman was looking very serious as she reported from a city street.

Jack settled in to listen, and his heart almost came out of his chest as he heard, ". . . Police say that they have no leads. The daughter of W. D. Herties was last seen a week ago, when she attended a girls' night out at the college. Sources close to the Herties family report that the head of the Herties real estate empire has been tight-lipped about his daughter's disappearance and has not been co-operating with police in their efforts.

"While there have been suggestions that there may have been foul play involved, the family refuses to confirm or deny any of these reports. We will continue to follow this story, Dave, and will get back to you if anything develops."

A talking male head appeared on the screen in front of the station logo.

"That was Rebecca Li, reporting from in front of the Herties Tower downtown. When we return, local weather with . . ."

Jack turned off the television.

"Well, so much for secrecy. I wonder what our caller will think of that," he asked.

"Probably won't even see it. He'll be too busy, doing whatever those guys do the night before the big trade."

"And what if the thing they do is watch the news?" Jack asked.

Valerie shrugged. "I guess we'll know soon enough," she said.

"I really want to get this guy," Jack said. "I don't just want the happy reunion between Jennifer and her father. I want this guy under lock and key. I want him to know that his plan didn't work and that you just can't get away with this kind of thing."

"You've convinced me, Jack." Valerie turned toward the man sulking on her couch. "I'm afraid, though, that it's looking more and more like he will get away with it, unless something happens. I think we have reached the stage where we need to take some action," she said. "I'm calling Keegan Willis."

"And just what is that going to prove?" Jack asked. "Calling Willis is only going to stir things up more. You know what he's like."

Valerie's frustration was evident on her face. Wrinkles appeared where there had been none so far that evening. The smile was gone. She was all business.

"There comes a point where I have to start acting like a cop, Jack. Much as I'd like to do it all your way, I feel a certain obligation to use my head and overrule my heart. This guy is going to leave home to pick up the cash tomorrow, right?"

"Well, yeah," Jack answered with a tone that said, *What a dumb question that was.*

"Okay. You are fairly certain this guy Fretz is the one doing all the calling. How about we check out his place while he's away? Nothing illegal with doing an outside check on the place. Knock on a few windows. Talk to a few neighbors. You let me know when this bozo is dropping by the pay phone, and I'll arrange for a cruiser to do a community security check. Let's see what we can do."

"He said no police," Jack reminded her.

"He won't see any police." A deepening redness in Valerie's face reflected her increasing level of frustration. "He'll be off making his million while we're doing our check. If it will make you feel any better, we can make sure to use an unmarked car."

"I don't know." Jack was not going to be easily convinced. He looked at the blank TV screen.

Valerie said nothing else but rose and went to where the phone was lying on the kitchen counter. She picked it up and began pushing buttons. She listened for a moment.

"Hi, Keegan? Valerie Cummins here. Yeah, fine. How about you? Good. Listen. I'm sorry to bother you at home, but I've got something I need to run by you . . . Yeah, I saw the news report. That's what I'm calling about . . . No, I haven't called Ted. I thought maybe we might need to do some extracurricular police work . . ."

Valerie walked down the hall with the phone, and Jack could no longer make out what was being said. He was starting to feel sorry for himself. It seemed to him as if he was losing control. He started to have visions of the whole thing going terribly wrong and of Herties blaming him for his daughter suffering a horrible fate.

Valerie returned a short while later and placed the phone on the coffee table in front of them. She turned to Jack.

"Now, listen. I did what I had to do. I'm not stupid. And I am charged with protecting the community. I can't go against my better judgment. I especially can't be controlled by some creep who has his own agenda."

"Oh, thanks for the vote of confidence," Jack said, his face shrouded by a dark cloud of self-pity.

"Not you! The guy who took Jennifer Herties," Valerie said. "We can't let him be in the driver's seat much longer, or he'll take us all places we don't want to go. I've got Keegan's support. He's going to take care of a few things tomorrow. All you have to do is let us know when the drop is going to take place. You'll call me on my cell. I don't think this guy is well connected enough to be able to monitor calls, but it's no use taking chances. I'll call Willis, and he'll put our plan into action. Simple as that. Nothing to worry about."

"That's easy for you to say." Jack had the look of a lost puppy.

"Yes, it is. And it's true. Trust me."

He still didn't look convinced. He slouched on the couch so his chin rested on his chest. His dejection was obvious.

Valerie spent the next little while trying to lift Jack's spirits, but it was clear that the concern about the next day weighed heavily on his mind. This was not a night for pleasant conversation.

"I wonder how the media found out about this," Jack asked finally.

"Hard to tell. The Herties empire is a big one. News travels. Some little comment. An aside to a trusted associate, and the story gets out—especially if you tag it with, 'and no one is to know.' "

"You don't think it was someone from detective division?" Jack asked.

"Give Willis a little credit, would you, Jack."

"Sorry. It was just a thought."

"Humph!" Valerie crossed her arms and stared at the floor.

"Aw, jeez, Val. I'm sorry. I didn't mean for us to end up mad at one another. You made such a great dinner, and we were getting along so well. Now look at what I've done. You're feeling angry. My emotions are shot. This guy's upset the apple cart for more than just Herties. I promise I'll be happier after all this is over."

Before Valerie could answer, the phone rang. She grabbed it.

It was Eric, and he wanted Jack.

"Hello," Jack said when Valerie handed him the phone.

"Jack. He called again. He is really put out with

whoever it was who leaked the story about Jennifer to the television people.

"He accused Herties of letting the story out so the police would know. Accused me of proving I was a wolf in sheep's clothing. Threatened to do something nasty if I didn't smarten up. He said that things would have to be done differently now, that Jennifer would not have as comfortable a night as she might have had otherwise. He told me to be ready to move quickly when he calls in the morning."

Jack shook his head as he heard all this. Valerie watched with apprehension on her face.

"I wonder what that means?" Jack asked.

"I have no idea. Look, I'm sorry. I hope I haven't said or done anything to mess up this thing."

"Hey, it wasn't you who let the story out. You've been playing the game with this guy for three or four days now. I can't think of any place where you might have screwed up. Don't be so hard on yourself."

"Sounds familiar," Valerie whispered with a smile.

"Thanks, Jack," Eric said. "I appreciate the support."

Jack looked at Valerie, and she blew him a kiss. He smiled for the first time in a while that evening.

"Eric, he used that phrase again, did he? You're sure those were his words?"

"Absolutely," Eric said. "I've been extra careful to be listening to every word. By the way, I've got a few tapes of the conversations I've been having with him. Nothing I haven't shared with you, but you should probably give them a listen tomorrow morning. They're all short and sweet."

"Listen, Eric," Jack said. "Have those things ready in the morning. I'll be bringing Herties to your place to be ready for the call. We'll get there around nine, and you can play the tapes. It will save me having to remember details to share with him. Maybe he'll pick up on something we've missed."

Jack's demeanor had changed. That was evident to Valerie. He was happiest when things were happening or getting ready to happen. He liked solving puzzles.

Jack made further plans with Eric for the morning and hung up. He turned to Valerie.

"I gather your guy watches the news," she said.

"Yeah. And he apparently doesn't have a lot of faith in Herties. He seems to be repeatedly accusing him of underhanded practices. I guess he figures Herties is making his fortune by other than honest means.

"We're going to play the tapes for W. D. in the morning," Jack continued. "We'll see whether he can get something from them that will help us confirm who the abductor is."

"Well, Jack," Valerie said, at last, "It's getting late, and I have to get up for work in the morning. So do you. Time to call it a night, I'm afraid."

"Yeah, I guess you're right. I always have the idea that if I don't go to bed, the morning won't come as soon. It never works quite that way."

"I'm sure it doesn't. You sure have some strange ideas," Valerie said.

Jack said good night and was soon on his way after assuring Valerie that he would call her once he knew the exact time that Herties was expected to leave the money for the exchange.

His mind was racing as he drove to the outskirts of town. He was certain that Fretz had taken Jennifer and that she was likely hidden away in his home.

He was concerned by what Eric had reported. The caller had said that the girl's evening would not be as comfortable as it might have been if the media had not caught wind of her disappearance. He wondered just what that might mean. He hoped that no harm would come to the girl before she could be rescued.

He parked and went directly to his apartment. There were no messages on his answering machine. A good sign, he supposed, since it meant that Eric had not been trying to get him since the call to Valerie's apartment.

It was late but not so late that he could not call Herties and confirm the time he would pick him up in the morning for the trip to Eric's.

The phone was answered on the first ring.

"Good evening, sir. I hope I haven't wakened you."

"Oh, hi, Jack. No, I haven't gone to bed yet. I'm a little concerned that I might not sleep, even when I do. I'm getting a little nervous about the whole thing. I'm praying that nothing goes wrong between now and the morning."

"Did you happen to be watching the news earlier this evening?"

"No. Why?"

Jack told him about the report of Jennifer's disappearance and the angry call that Eric had received a little later.

"I'm not sure what the kidnapper has planned for your daughter tonight. It sounds like he's considering moving her to a more secure but less comfortable location. I wish I could be a little more encouraging. I don't think he intends to do her any harm, but I can't be sure.

"I think I might know who our man is," Jack said. "Forgive me if I don't say who at the moment. I want you to hear some tapes we've made. After you've had a chance to listen to them, maybe you can confirm our suspicions.

"I need to tell you that the police will be doing some investigative work while we are waiting for the exchange. We need to be able to prove that this guy is who we think he is."

"I really wish you wouldn't be so secretive with me." Herties sounded anguished by Jack's revelations. "I'm beginning to think we might have done other things to ensure Jen's safety."

"Sir, trust me. We've done everything we could, short of having the police become fully involved."

"Maybe we shouldn't have drawn up short of bringing them online with us." Herties sounded frightened and frustrated.

"They know the situation. They are at the ready, once things begin to happen. We had to keep them out of it, for your daughter's sake. We had to take her abductor at his word," Jack said.

"I hope you're right."

I hope I'm right too, Jack thought.

He said, "Well, sir, I'll see you at eight in the morning at your office. We'll drive out to my friend's home and let you listen to those tapes. After that, we'll have to wait for the kidnapper to make the next move."

"I'll be waiting for you, Jack. Don't be late."

After he had hung up, Jack paced around the apartment, thinking about the plans for the next day and wondering again if anything had been missed.

He sat down with the notes he had made after his interviews with the various suspects. One by one, he checked them off after considering all the alternatives. He was left with only one suspect.

What if the police were to storm the house tonight? If they found the girl, all well and good. If Jack was wrong, there would be consequences. If he was right, but the girl was somewhere else, the consequences might be worse for Jennifer Herties. It would take more than a suspicion to get the wheels in motion.

He would try to sleep and see what the morning would bring. He suspected that that would be easier said than done.

He was right.

Jack tossed and turned in his bed through the night. Thoughts of the coming day continued to disturb his dreams. Fear of failure and of the whole affair turning nasty made it impossible for him to have any calmness of soul.

He got up and paced for a while. He tried to watch TV. That definitely did not help. All that he could find were programs trying to sell him salad bowls, knives, and exercise gear. Or old movies that featured gangsters, monsters, or well-trained animals performing impossible feats of bravery.

He reviewed his notes again and asked himself over and over whether he could have prepared better.

Of course you could have made better plans. Of course you could have done a better job of protecting that young girl. There's a whole lot of stuff you could have done better, but you didn't. You did the best you could, now live with the consequences. Jack would argue with himself like this a number of times before sunrise. He knew too that no matter how this situation resolved itself, he'd still be asking the questions long afterward.

Chapter Fifteen
The Best Laid Plans

Jack closed his eyes. When he opened them again, the sun was rising and the clock warned that if he didn't get moving soon, he'd be late for his appointment to pick up W. D. Herties. He was fully awake as he rushed around his apartment. No time for a leisurely coffee and the morning news. He had to be on his way at once.

Jack hated this sort of a start to his day, especially one as important as this one. The inside of his mouth felt like the underside of a camel saddle. At least, that was his assumption, having never had any intimate contact with either a camel or its saddle.

His clothes didn't feel right. He had just pulled on pants and shirt, socks and shoes, and headed out the door with his coat and an old file folder containing the details of the Herties case.

As always happened when he had to flee his home

without being able to indulge some of his obsessive-compulsive behaviors, Jack felt certain he had forgotten something. He was sure he had either left something behind or neglected to lock a door or turn off an appliance. He comforted himself in the assurance that he had not turned on the coffee maker, so that was safe. He hadn't had time to shave, so the electric razor was unplugged. He hadn't been to his office in days, so the door was still locked. Then he began to worry about whether there was important mail in the office, which he hadn't seen. Were there unanswered messages on the office answering machine?

He debated with himself right up to the doors of the Herties Tower. He parked by the curb and ran inside, where he asked the man at the security desk to call up for Mr. Herties.

The uniformed guard proceeded to inform Jack that Mr. Herties did not take kindly to people calling up from the lobby. He looked at his clipboard and informed Jack that his name did not appear on the list of people who were expected. In fact, "Mr. Herties is not expecting anyone in his office today. You'll have to wait for his secretary to come in at nine. You might be able to make an appointment then."

The guard had a smug look on his face, which Jack would dearly have loved to remove with the back of his hand.

Jack fumbled in his pocket for Herties office number and was dialing his cell phone when the elevator doors opened and out walked his morning passenger. He was carrying a hefty-looking metal briefcase.

Herties nodded to the security officer and went immediately to Jack's side.

"Why didn't you have me paged? I would have come straight down. We need to be on our way," Herties asked.

Jack could see that the guard was paying particular attention to the multimillionaire's words. There was a worried look on his face. It was apparent; he knew he had somehow made a serious error in judgment.

"I just got here. This gentleman was about to let me go up to get you."

Jack smiled at the man behind the desk. *One never knows when a debt owed might come in handy,* he thought.

The guard smiled back and nodded his thanks that he would live to protect the building for another day. He watched as the two men left the building.

As they approached the car, Jack could see a woman in another sort of uniform, with a pad in her hand, taking particular note of his license.

"Great. Just what I need on a day like today," Jack said. Frustration filled his voice.

"Let me take care of this," Herties said as he strode up behind the young woman.

"Good morning, Miss. Lovely day today."

"This your car?" She was getting right to the point.

"As a matter of fact, no, it's not. It belongs to my friend Jack, here." He indicated the man standing with him.

"This is a private no-parking zone. You can't park here." She was looking at Jack now.

"Do you know who I am?" Herties asked.

"Can't say that I do. Doesn't much matter, though. My business is with your friend. When I'm done, his business will be with the folks I work for, who are in charge of monitoring the parking around the building."

"Well, Miss, unless you are tired of working for them, you had better know that I am W. D. Herties. You might have heard of me in your travels. I want to say, first off, that I appreciate the fine job you are doing to keep the entryway clear in front of my building. But I also need to let you know that when you deal with the public, it has been my experience that if you exercise a little bit of courtesy, your relationships will be much happier.

"It comes down to this. Your company works for me. You work for them. So, we might say that indirectly I pay your salary. Would you like to cancel that ticket? Please?" He smiled.

"Mr. Herties, I'm sorry," the woman stammered. "I didn't know. If I had known . . ."

"That's the problem, isn't it?" Herties said. "We never know. You can't ever be sure who you are talking to in your business. It's always best to leave a good impression from the beginning.

"Now, I usually charge five thousand dollars a session to pass out that kind of advice. But you look like a smart girl who can learn a lesson without having to be told twice. I'll give you this session for free. Now, just give me that ticket and call off your tow truck, and we'll call it square."

The girl tore off the ticket, ripped it in half, and handed it to Herties.

"Thank you. Have a good day," he said cheerily.

"You too, sir," the girl replied and moved along the sidewalk, speaking into the microphone that was clipped to the shoulder of her uniform.

After they had settled in the car, Herties turned to Jack.

"I'm sorry to have taken so much time with the girl. I know we are in somewhat of a hurry, but I felt the situation needed a firm hand. Even if it had been someone who decided to blatantly ignore the signs, there's no excuse for lack of respect. It reflects poorly on me when those who work for me aren't polite, no matter that it is at arm's length.

"I hope she gets her wish," he added.

"What's that, sir?" Jack asked, pulling into the flow of traffic.

"That I have a good day. I want my daughter back in one piece. I wouldn't mind being able to retrieve this too." He patted the brief case on his lap. "But it's far less important than Jennifer's life. If this works out well, I think I'll give all of it to charity," he added.

Jack kept a close eye on the traffic as he drove. He was well aware that he was carrying valuable cargo. He didn't want to mess things up at this stage in the game.

Fortunately, traffic was lighter leaving the city at this time of day.

"We're headed to the suburbs, sir. My friend Eric lives over there. You met him on Friday. He's been taking the calls intended for you. We've been taping the conversations.

There isn't a whole lot of information on them, from what I can gather, but the guy has said some intriguing things and made some backhanded references that we think might help you decide whether he's someone you know."

"And your friend has been getting the calls because . . ."

"As I think I mentioned on Saturday, the guy who has your daughter has your business card. It is one of the old ones with the misprint. By dialing the wrong number, he connected with Eric."

"And we didn't set him straight. Why?" Herties asked.

"His first contact was a threat and a cryptic message. Eric had no chance to set him straight, as far as the number was concerned. I think doing so might have spooked the guy and, if he realized he might have ruined his plans, he could have hurt your daughter.

"When we heard that he didn't want you contacting the police, my friend Val suggested that we could make some preliminary enquiries without it ever appearing that you were doing so."

Jack continued, "Your friend the police chief has been brought up to speed on all this and has been careful not to be seen with you. Because you haven't been able to submit anything other than a missing persons report, our friends have been somewhat hamstrung in their investigation but have nevertheless been on the alert for breaking developments."

"It sounds too complicated for my liking," Herties said. "I hope all of this works. I don't know what I'll do if Jen is hurt. I have no idea what her mother will think when she hears about it all."

"If all goes the way we plan, you'll be able to tell her

that the problem was solved, and you can all have a happy reunion when your wife gets back from her trip."

They were approaching Eric's apartment building, and Jack stopped by the main entrance.

"I'll drop you off here. Do you think your briefcase is safe with you?" Jack asked.

"I'd feel more secure having it with me. Yes. Thanks," the millionaire replied.

Jack let his passenger out by the door to the apartment building with the promise to be right back. He parked his car and jogged back to the main entrance. The two men were soon admitted to the building.

They rode the elevator to Eric's floor and were met in the hallway by their host for the next couple of hours.

"Any calls yet?" Jack asked.

"Not a peep," Eric replied. "I suspect that when things start happening, they will move pretty quickly, though. You guys want coffee?"

"I'm dying for a cup," Jack said with enthusiasm. "I didn't have a chance to get any before I left home."

Herties said he would have just one cup.

"I've been drinking the stuff since I got up at five, and I think I'm about to reach my limit," he added.

Eric asked, "What's the plan, Jack?"

"I'd like to listen to the tapes you've made. They may not mean a whole lot to me, but perhaps Mr. Herties can pull something out of what is being said that will help us track down this guy."

"I've got them right here, and I've got a player that can

handle the little cassettes. The speed is a little different, but the guy is disguising his voice, in any case. At least you can hear the conversation."

"Let's hear them," Jack said.

Eric put a tape in the hand-held player and laid it on the coffee table. The three men hunched around the little device to hear what was being said. The tape was playing at a speed faster than that at which it was recorded, so the pitch of the two voices was a little higher.

Recordings of the earlier conversations had not been made, so what were being heard were mostly details from the last couple of days. Herties listened intently and frowned whenever his daughter's name was mentioned by the kidnapper.

The conversation on the tape was just about at an end. The caller was rehashing the details of the planned drop and reminding his listener to be by the phone at exactly 10:00 on Monday.

". . . Don't try to put anything over on me. I know you're a wolf in sheep's clothing and I . . ."

"Play that back," Herties yelled.

Eric obediently rewound the tape a little and played it again.

". . . I know you're a wolf in sheep's clothing and . . ."

"I know who that is. I'm almost positive that's Bernard Fretz." Herties was clearly excited about the revelation.

"How can you be so sure?" Jack asked.

"It's my name. Fretz is one of the few people who knows my real name. He used to tease me about it. I don't know why he's doing this. It's a dead giveaway."

"Can you explain this for us, please? I'm a little confused," Jack said.

Eric moved closer to the front edge of the couch and focused all his attention on Herties.

"W. D. It stands for Wolfgang Donald. I know it's silly, but I did not want to be called Wolfgang. It is part of my German heritage, but I just never liked the name. And then, I must humbly admit, I am a very rich man. I did not want to use my second name and be referred as The Canadian Donald every time I was mentioned in the media.

"Fretz found out one day when he was doing some accounts. He mentioned to me that he had 'broken the code,' so to speak. We came to a mutual agreement. He would never refer to me as other than W. D. in public, and when we were speaking on a social basis, he could only call me Wolf. He has kept his promise to this day, as far as I know. I suppose he's angry about being let go. But he was found skimming those funds, and I just couldn't allow that to pass."

"Mr. Herties, that is a confirmation of what I suspected after my talk with Fretz yesterday. When all this is over, perhaps we should visit the matter of who was skimming the money. I have some thoughts on that, too, but this is the wrong time. We have other, more pressing matters to deal with right now. And yes, I'm certain Fretz is angry, and that is the reason you are being put through all this."

Herties lowered his face into his hands and sat, unmoving, for a time.

"You think he's doing this, and dropping those hints to let me know that it's him? He thinks that he won't get caught?" Herties asked.

"I think he wants you to know who he is," Jack said. "I think that, in the heat of his anger, he is definitely not thinking straight. He will get caught, but his mind is dulled to the severity of what he has done. He will be going to jail as soon as he's caught. But first we have to get Jennifer back."

Jack immediately called Valerie and told her that the police should expect to be arresting Fretz for the kidnapping. He promised to call again as soon as they had received the details of the drop.

Eric continued to play the tape for Jack and Herties. There was not much new information. All that remained was the waiting for the call that would hopefully set the final scenes in motion.

At ten, Eric's phone rang. He picked it up.

"Herties here." W. D. looked a little startled to hear his own name, but gave a tight smile when the truth hit him.

Eric listened. He made notes as the caller apparently continued to speak.

He wrote "The Corners Mall" and circled it. His next note was "10:20 by pay phone outside drugstore. Wait for call."

Finally, he said, "Yes, I understand," and hung up.

The two others leaned closer for a recap of the details.

"We need to be at the phone booth at the minimall by twenty past. He's going to call and give further details. He reminded me that he doesn't want to see any police or the deal is off."

"Let's go," Jack said, heading for the door. We've got about fifteen minutes. Eric, you'll need to wait here. I'm playing chauffeur to Mr. Herties, and there can't be anyone else in the backseat with him. I'll let you know as soon as everything is settled."

"I really appreciate your help, Eric," Herties said, shaking the man's hand vigorously. "When all this is over, I'll find a way to pay you back."

With that, the two men were gone and heading for the elevator. Herties had his case firmly in hand. He looked like any other businessman on his way out to work.

Jack escorted Herties to the car this time and opened the back door.

"Got to make this look authentic," he said as he closed the door after his passenger. Then he got into the front seat and dug around in the glove compartment. He extracted a chauffeur's cap, which he planted on his head. He started the engine and drove off to the location they had been given, further to the west.

"I'll stop by the phone," Jack said as he drove. "I'll roll down the window in the back so you can hear when it rings. Get out. Identify yourself, and just listen. Take notes about the directions, and get back in."

Herties patted his pockets and reached inside his jacket. He extracted a leather-covered notepad. He reached into a shirt pocket and retrieved a pen.

"All set," he said.

"I appreciate how calm you are in all this, sir," Jack said over his shoulder.

"The only way I can keep calm is to look at this like a business negotiation. If I stop to think about what I'm really doing, I won't make it."

"Good enough. Once we have the instructions, I'll

drive you to wherever we have to go. We'll do whatever he asks and hopefully have your daughter home by lunch.

"Excuse me while I make a call," Jack said, grabbing his cell phone from the console between the front seats.

Jack dialed Valerie's cell number and listened.

"We're on our way, Val. We're getting further instructions at twenty past. He'll be watching us, so Brown, Willis, and the rest can make a fast sweep of his place. Call my cell if you get anything."

"Be careful" was all Valerie said. The line went dead.

Jack drove up the hill and turned into the little strip mall. A bank of pay phones sat just outside a small pharmacy at one end. A digital clock on the front of the building read 10:18.

Jack stopped in the parking lot and watched the clock.

"I figure this is the clock Fretz is watching too," he said to his backseat passenger. I'll try to time our stop at the phone to coincide with the change to twenty past. Don't say much. Just identify yourself. Let him do the talking. He could probably tell the difference between your voice and Eric's."

"But we've spoken before. In the office. How come . . ."

"Well, he didn't seem to pick up on Eric's voice in the past little while," Jack interrupted, aware that time was passing quickly. "Get ready."

The clock switched to 10:19, and Jack watched the sweep hand on his wristwatch. After twenty seconds, he pulled out of the parking space and slowly coasted up to the pay phones. He stopped and pressed the button to open the window in the back. The car stopped, and the phone immediately began to ring.

Herties got out of the car at once and picked up the receiver on the ringing phone.

"Herties," he said and listened. He made notes in his notebook. He hung up and returned to the car.

As he closed the door, he said, "There's an old building, a sort of community hall, along the road. It's painted light blue."

"I know the place," Jack said and put the car in gear.

"We are to pull into the parking lot, and I'm to put the money under the stairs around the side. We have to go down the road the way we came until we come to a big church. We wait in the parking lot. Jen will come to us there."

Jack pulled out of the mall and headed along the road to the location Herties had been given. The building was old and in need of repair. It sat on a large lot with a treed area on one side. A set of stairs led up to a service entrance away from the road.

Jack carefully maneuvered his car onto the gravel drive and drew up beside the wooden stairs. Again Herties exited alone, this time taking the case with him. He slid it under the stairs and out of view. He looked around to make sure no passersby could see what he was doing. Then he returned to the car.

Jack drifted away from the building and headed down the block to the church. From the parking lot there, it was impossible to see the building they had just come from, but it was only a couple of minutes' walk.

Jack turned off the engine.

"Now we just have to wait," he said, and turned around to look at Wolf Herties.

The man was biting his lip. His forehead was furrowed. He looked small and old in the backseat of a car that he would not choose to ride in, if given the option.

"I hope he hasn't been abusing my girl. If he has, I'll use every influence I have to make sure he . . ."

"I'm sure your daughter will be just fine. It shouldn't be too long now."

They waited.

More than an hour had passed, and it was becoming apparent to Jack that he had been wrong. There was no sign of the girl. What should he do?

He called Valerie first.

"Listen, Jack. I've been on traffic patrol. I haven't had a chance to check back with our guys. Give me a few minutes. I'll call you right back."

Jack relayed the message to Herties, and they waited for Valerie to report.

"He's killed my daughter and taken my money. Now he'll catch a plane and leave town for some place where he can't be brought to justice." Herties was becoming frantic.

"I'm sure she's fine," Jack said, although he wasn't at all sure that she was even alive.

The ringing of Jack's cell phone startled both men.

"Hi, Jack. Valerie, here. Bad news."

Chapter Sixteen
She's All Tied up

Jack tried to sound calm. He could feel the hairs beginning to stand up on the back of his neck.

"Go on," he said.

"The team went up to the house. No one was there. No sign of the girl. There was some scrap wood around the back. Looked like someone was building something. They couldn't be sure what. And Jack . . ."

"Yes?"

"They found a shovel. It was one of those long spades that are used to dig graves. It doesn't look good, Jack."

"Thanks, Valerie. Mr. Herties and I are at the church down the road from the minimall, waiting for Jennifer to show. Talk to you later." He tried to cover his fear and disappointment, for the sake of the girl's father.

"Apparently, Jennifer is no longer at Fretz's house. She must be with him." Jack was not about to dash the man's hopes without some concrete evidence.

"I'm going to call Eric and see if he's heard anything," he added.

Jack got out of the car and walked away a short distance. When he got through to Eric, it was apparent that things were not as they should be.

"What on earth happened?" Eric fairly shouted into the phone.

"What do you mean, 'what happened'? We left the money, and we waited, and waited some more. The girl never showed up. He called, didn't he?"

"Oh, yeah, you can bet he did," Eric said, his tone a mixture of frustration and panic. "He went on at length about how I had betrayed him and had called the cops."

If Herties had been looking, the expression on Jack's face would have alerted him at once that there was something terribly wrong. Jack hoped that with his back to the car, he could hide his shock.

"What is that supposed to mean?" he asked, frustration mounting. "Is he still upset about the news last night? I thought you had sorted that all out."

"It wasn't that. He said he saw the police waiting by the side of the road across from the drop. He accused me of setting him up. Jack, he is far from being a happy camper, if you get my drift. You've got to fix this, and fast."

"You told him that we, or rather you, had not called the police, or asked them to set up surveillance. You told him you had been playing by his rules."

"I felt a little out of the loop about most of what was happening. I didn't know where you were, or what the pickup plans were, after you left the minimall. It was kind of scary, Jack.

"And yes," Eric continued. "I assumed that you wouldn't have done something that stupid. So I told him I was completely dumbfounded about the whole mess. I asked him what he wanted me to do now."

Jack walked further from the car to a place where the view from the backseat was blocked by a large oak. He leaned on the tree and heaved a sigh.

"And, what happens now?" he asked. He looked at the ground and shook his head. Dejection was written on his face.

"He's going to call back," Eric replied. "He said he had to think about this."

"Did he get the money? Is the girl safe? Do we wait here?" Jack sounded frantic.

"No. I don't think he got the money. He said he just drove right by when he saw I had betrayed him. I guess it's still there. Jeez, I hope it's still there, Jack. He said that I was making it tough for him to keep the girl in good condition. *Unscarred* was the word he used.

"He thinks Herties is at home. Figures that after the drop, he got away from the action to let the police take over. You don't need to wait there. You might want to go back and look for that briefcase."

"Now, there is an understatement if I ever heard one," Jack said, turning and heading back to his car. Wolf Herties was going to be one angry dog. That was for sure.

He stopped midway in the parking lot. It was empty except for his car. Pulling out his phone again, he keyed Valerie's cell number. Once more, he turned away from the vehicle.

"Val, it didn't go down the way we expected. I don't

have time to talk right now, but can you do a little snooping for me? Should be relatively easy, but only you can do it."

"That's awful, Jack. I'm so sorry. Is the girl still okay?" the female officer asked.

"As far as we know. Yes. Can you find out why a patrol car would be out in front of the community hall at about half past ten this morning?"

"Aw, nuts. And that was the pickup spot I suppose. Darn!" she said. "Okay, give me a few minutes. I'll check with my folks in traffic division and see if we had a car out there. I'll call you back. You're on your cell?"

"Yeah, I'm out here with Herties. We were waiting for his daughter to materialize."

"I'll get back to you."

Jack walked back to the car and got in. He turned and faced Wolf Herties.

"Sir, it looks like we won't be seeing your daughter today."

The man looked stricken. The skin on his face sagged like a wet paper towel.

"My God, what's happened?"

"As far as we can tell, she's safe. Fretz was scared off by a stray police car that just happened to be in the wrong place. He thinks you crossed him. It's going to take just a little longer to get her back."

"I want to talk to her. I need to know she's all right. I need . . ." It was evident that all the money in the world couldn't buy comfort now for a man who wanted his child back.

"Right now, you need to retrieve your money, and I

need to get you home or at least to someplace safe and out of the public eye."

Jack started the car and eased out of the parking lot. He headed back to the hall where the cash had been left. There were no police in sight now. The gravel drive was empty as well. He pulled up to the service entrance, being careful to block any view from the street.

"Wait here," he said to Herties and opened his door. He felt under the stairs and grabbed the handle of the case. He pulled it out and carried it to the back door of the car. Opening the door, he laid it on the seat beside his passenger. He closed the door and climbed into the front of the car again.

"I think we had better stop at Eric's. If Fretz calls, you can at least hear the conversation firsthand. I doubt that you'd be able to concentrate very well at the office, in any case."

"I guess you're right, Jack," the distraught father said. "This whole thing is not turning out the way I had hoped."

"It's not working out the way any of us had suspected. That's for sure," Jack said.

Neither man spoke for the rest of the trip.

Ten minutes later, they were back to the place where they had all started the day together. Herties sat in an easy chair with the case full of money by his side. Jack was in the kitchen, trying to get Eric's old kettle to boil for tea. Eric was hovering over a pot of soup on the stove. Apart from the noises of meal preparation and the ticking of a battery-powered clock on the living room wall, everything was quiet.

"I want to talk to my daughter," Herties said after a few moments.

"You said that's what you wanted back in the parking lot," Jack said. "When Fretz calls again, Eric will tell him that's what you want. He'll tell him you want proof that she is alive, and we'll get him to put her on the phone."

Jack turned to Eric, who was ladling soup into bowls. "You've got caller ID, don't you?"

"Sorry, Jack. I don't. Never had much need for it. I called the phone company to ask about it once. They said that they could get things set up for me in about a week. Then they told me the price, and I figured I had better uses for my money. I can usually figure out who's calling by the time they've said hello. At least, there hasn't been much use for it—until now."

"It might have been helpful," Jack said. "I was thinking, it might tell us if Fretz had moved his base of operations after that little mess-up this morning. I guess we'll just have to play it by ear.

"As long as he's still ready to bargain, we'll, at least, get your daughter back, sir," he said, looking at the drawn and disheveled Herties.

Eric served the soup along with some sandwiches he had made. Jack had been able to make the kettle function, and there was tea for them to drink.

When they were settled, Eric turned to Jack.

"Do you suppose that you'll get Jennifer back safely?" he asked.

Jack shot him a glance that would cut through metal. Eric caught the significance of the look, but now it was too late.

Jack tried to cover.

"Of course we will. Jennifer is in no apparent danger. Fretz doesn't intend her any harm, he just wants the money. Once he has that, he plans to leave on the next plane. He said he had sold his house, but I'm not so sure that wasn't just to throw us off his scent."

At the back of his mind was the image of cut wood and the gravedigger's shovel that the police had uncovered in their search of Fretz's home on the mountain.

Herties was clearly distraught. Jack dearly wished that he could give him better assurances than he had. He wasn't sure whether he had succeeded in convincing the man of the ultimate success of their plan.

The rest of the meal was spent in relative silence, except for the asking for and receiving of food and drink, salt and pepper, cream and sugar.

The rationalizing was over. The plan had been executed as written. A single unknown factor had crept into the mix. Now they were back to where they had been twenty-four hours earlier.

Eventually, Valerie called Jack on his cell phone.

"It was just a standard traffic check, Jack," she said. "One of our guys was out there with the radar gun, looking for speeders. He caught a few. He didn't notice anything suspicious. He must have pulled up just after you two guys left."

"Well, thanks for the info," Jack said. "It doesn't change things much, but maybe we can sound more convincing when we're telling this guy we had nothing to do with it."

"Jack, I've been talking to Willis too," Valerie added.

"He was all set to run up the hill and chain the guy to a tree for target practice. I managed to talk him out of it, but he's taken a few precautions you should know about."

"Should I?" Jack walked down the hall, away from the other two men.

"He thought it wise to send an unmarked patrol into the community. It's down the hill from Fretz's house, where he can't see it. They can't see him, either, but he has to pass their location to come and go in his vehicle. His truck isn't in the driveway. They checked. He's obviously been using a pay phone, or a cell phone, to talk to you today."

"Where is he now?" Jack asked, keeping his voice low.

"They don't know. They only set up the surveillance after they were sure he would be gone. He hasn't come back."

"I doubt that he'd use a pay phone when he can call from just about anywhere with a cell phone," Jack said. "That knowledge could come in handy."

"I'm off at four. Call me if you need me. Gotta go."

Jack could hear the wail of a siren coming over the phone. Valerie's voice in the distance was reading a license number into her police radio. She had obviously just tossed her cell phone on the seat when the speeder went by her location and had forgotten to turn it off.

Jack folded his own phone and placed it in his pocket. He returned to the other two who were sitting and sipping their tea. He didn't feel any urgency to share the contents of his phone conversation with them just yet.

Chapter Seventeen
Boxed in

The shadows were lengthening, and Jack was beginning to despair of hearing from Fretz, when the phone began to ring. He motioned for Eric to answer it and handed it to him.

"Herties here," he said, looking off into space. He listened and then said, "Look, I had nothing to do with that police car being there."

Jack had told the men what Valerie had reported about the traffic check. Eric relayed the information to the caller.

"Look. I want to talk to my daughter," he said. "I want to know that she is safe. If I don't hear her voice, the deal is off."

Jack quietly applauded his friend's bravery in standing up to the kidnapper.

Eric listened to the answer to his request.

"Alright, then. I'll be waiting. Good-bye." He hung up and handed the phone back to Jack.

"What did he say?" the other two men asked, almost in unison.

"He has not gone home," Eric said. "Jennifer is hidden somewhere, in a safe place. Or so he says. He has to go to where she is and take her a phone. She will call you, I mean me, later tonight." Then he added, "I wonder why she can't call back within the hour?"

"He's probably afraid of being seen in broad daylight and wants to make sure he's not being tailed," Jack suggested. "He doesn't trust you and isn't completely convinced you didn't put that cop on the corner this morning."

Herties looked at his watch.

"I assume it's okay if I stay here until she calls," he said. "I really do want to talk to her. I need to hear her voice. It wouldn't be the same to just have you report that she had called here."

"Sir, I'd be happy to let you stay here as long as you would like," Eric said. "My accommodations are rather humble, but feel free to make yourself at home."

"Thank you. Thank you so much. You are very generous," the millionaire said. "Now, if you would allow me, I'd like to make a couple of phone calls. The first will be to Bett at the office. She can have calls transferred to my cell phone. The second might appeal to the two of you. I haven't had much to eat today and though your sandwiches and soup were great, I'm feeling the need for something a little more substantial about now. I'd like to order us all some supper."

Eric and Jack agreed that it was a fine plan. Eric was particularly relieved, knowing that his cupboard was far too bare to sustain the three of them for much longer.

Herties made his calls.

Bett was glad to hear from him and reported that all had gone well at the office that day. She would have the call forwarding activated at once and hoped to see him in the morning.

The second call was to a caterer that the millionaire particularly liked who would do up a small order and deliver it to him anywhere in town, knowing that when he had an expansive affair in the works, they would be called upon to cater that too. They promised to have a man at Eric's door within the hour.

"Well, now all we have left to do is wait," Herties said, picking up the case and opening it.

Jack and Eric could see neat packages of bills filling the interior. It was more money than they had ever seen in one place or might expect to ever see again.

By way of explanation, Herties said, "I put my cell phone in here after we picked this up again. I'll keep it out now, in case any calls come for me."

Herties had said, "All we have to do now is wait." And that was precisely what they did.

The wait for their meal was not a lengthy one. The food was delivered within the hour. Eric went to great pains to apologize to his rich guest about the state of his china and the mismatched flatware that he kept jumbled in a kitchen drawer. He had had to search for a third knife before they could settle down to the meal.

For his part, Wolf Herties was quite genial and seemed not a bit disturbed by the state of Eric's kitchen supplies.

The men ate in silence, as they had at the lunch meal.

Valerie would laugh at them as being typically male, Jack thought. More interested in the food than the fellowship would likely be her accusation.

Jack was deep in thought, though. He was worrying about what the outcome of all this would be. He figured that Herties likely had an opinion about all this too. But the millionaire was not sharing his thoughts at the moment. Jack didn't want to get him into too much rumination, lest he think himself into an unhealthy state of mind.

With the approaching night, the skies had darkened, and a torrential rain had begun to fall. A strong wind, typical for this time of year, was driving the rain against the windowpane. In the little apartment, it sounded like some small wild creature was trying to tear through the walls with its claws.

Various thoughts crept into Jack's mind. The old police mentality was beginning to take control. He explored the nooks and crannies of his mental data banks for some small piece of information that might help—might put them one step ahead of the man, so bent on teaching his former employer a lesson that he couldn't envision the other consequences of his actions.

"All we have to do now is wait," Herties had said, and a faraway voice in Jack's head was saying don't wait as it drew closer. Jack began to meditate on what it was they were supposed to be waiting for, and a small, faint, light began to glow. Maybe there was hope after all.

"I've got an idea," he said. "I've been thinking about the arrangements for tonight's phone call. It appears that Jennifer might not be with Fretz. I don't think she's at the house anymore, either."

"Is that significant?" Eric asked. Herties had a questioning look in his eyes too.

"If Fretz has Jennifer hidden away somewhere, he's not going to leave her where she can contact anyone. Even if she's tied up somewhere, he's likely not going to leave her alone with the means to communicate her location. If it's not his house, it's likely a shed somewhere, or a crawlspace, somewhere away from prying eyes and ears."

The looks from the other two asked so what?

"I think he's going to have to take a cell phone to her so she can call."

"Um, Jack. Even if you could get the number she is calling from, it's mobile. All you'll be able to track is the billing address." Herties gave Jack a look that conveyed a sudden lack of confidence.

"I think I have another little trick that will help us out," Jack said. "Let me make a call."

He picked up the portable phone and headed down the hall, dialing as he went.

The other two could hear him in conversation with someone but were unable to make out what Jack was saying.

"That would be great. I'll call you as soon as we're ready. Yeah, thanks." Jack was coming back down the hall. They could hear these last snippets of conversation, and then he hung up.

"All we have to do now is wait," Jack said. He smiled and sat down. He gave no response to the two sets of eyes that stared at him.

He looked from one to the other.

"All we have to do now is wait," he said again, and nothing more.

"You're a real help. You know that, Jack?" Herties face had fallen some more. The stress was clearly weighing heavily on him.

"I'd prefer not to get started on what I've arranged. I'm hoping that Jen will call soon, and the less you know right now, the less the likelihood you might say something to her that Fretz will pick up."

They seemed only moderately placated by the explanation, but let the subject drop.

Someone once said that the best-laid plans often go awry. It seemed like this day, it was Wolf Herties' turn. And it was about to get even more stressful before the day was out.

When the phone rang again, it was not Jennifer on the other end of the phone. Eric put the phone to his ear, and Herties leaned close to hear what was being said. He didn't need to.

Eric made gestures to indicate that it was Fretz who was calling. Had he not, Jack and Wolf Herties would soon have figured it out. The angry sound of the voice on the other end of the line was so loud that Eric had to hold the phone away from his ear. Herties backed away from the earpiece suddenly at the first outburst. The voice sounded distorted through the tiny earpiece.

Finally, Eric spoke to his caller. "I'm sorry to hear that. You realize you are not making any friends with this delay. You know that I know who you are and where you are. Why don't we call this thing off and be done with it?"

Evidently, that wasn't in the plan, and Fretz hung up.

The millionaire looked like a welfare case when Eric finally replaced the receiver.

"She won't be calling, at least not tonight," Eric said. "He says he had to make some changes in the plan, because he's afraid that there are police watching him. He says she's safe, and no harm will come to her, unless he finds out the authorities are involved."

"You're sure this plan of yours is going to work?" Herties asked.

Jack was holding his head in his hands when he replied, "Not tonight, it won't. But, yes, my friends are being very careful. Some folks who are involved don't even know what they are helping with, but they have resources ready for us to use when the time is right."

"Did he say anything else?" Herties asked, the panic becoming evident.

"He said I'd have to wait till morning. Jen will call me to let me know she's safe. Then I'm, I mean you, are to wait for a call from him about the drop. If all goes well, you'll get your daughter back. But he said this is the last chance."

"I'm so worried, Jack. I don't know what to do next," the millionaire said.

"Well, I guess the agenda is being set for us," Jack said. "He's got your daughter hidden away. She's not with him. Otherwise I'd suggest an all-points bulletin for the guy. As it is, if we catch him now, he might not tell us where Jen is, and it might take a while to get her back home."

"Sir, it's very late," Eric said. "I don't have much to

offer, but I do have a small guest room that you are welcome to use for the night. It will save you going back to town and then having to ride back here in the morning. I think that the money will be safe with you.

"There might be more danger of something happening if you had to take it back to town," he added.

"Why, thank you, Eric. That is very kind of you. I don't suppose I'm going to be getting much sleep tonight anyway. One place to lie down is as good as any other, and believe me, in spite of what you might think, this is a palace compared to some of the places I've been forced to lay my head."

"Then it's settled," Jack said. "You'll stay here until morning."

"Eric, would it be all right if I make this my base of operations for the night as well?" Jack asked. "All I need is your couch and a four-course breakfast in the morning."

"Use the couch. Scratch the breakfast," Eric replied. "I'll think of something, but don't expect gourmet food, Jack."

Eric showed Herties to the spare room, where he made sure the money was as safe as an apartment bedroom could make it. The case was slipped under the bed.

Jack busied himself calling someone—he didn't reveal who—and telling them that what they had planned was being put off till the next day.

"I'll get back to whoever is on shift at the time. You don't think there will be any problem with that? That will be great. Thanks. G'bye."

After he hung up, he looked at his watch and suddenly realized that he had not called Valerie.

Even though it was late, he knew she would want to hear what had happened. She would be expecting better news than Jack was about to offer.

He had underestimated what her response would be. He could hear the devastation in her voice. She was not that many years older than Jennifer, and Jack imagined that she was putting herself in the girl's place. For all her training as a peace officer, there would be nothing that could quite prepare man, or woman, for the sort of experience that the Herties girl was having at that moment.

"Jack, I feel so helpless. I'll do whatever I can but I'm tied up with work all day tomorrow. It's police work, but you know, given the choice, I'd rather be working your case. Call my cell, if you think I can help."

"Thanks, I appreciate that," Jack said. He bit his lip for a moment and added, "You told me once that you used to go to church a lot. It wouldn't hurt to offer up a prayer, or two, under the circumstances."

"I'll do that, Jack. Good luck in the morning. Remember to call me. A little earlier in the evening would be nice. Sleep tight."

"I doubt that," he replied and hung up the phone.

Jack sat on the couch and tapped nervously on the armrest as he waited for Eric to return from showing Herties his room. He laid his head back and closed his eyes. His mind was spinning.

Could anything else happen to make this mess worse? he wondered.

He didn't hear Eric come back into the room and was startled back to reality when he heard him speaking beside him.

"He's decided not to come back out for now. He looks just awful, Jack. He's going to need a vacation when this is all over. I can't imagine what it must be doing to him inside. I know what it's doing to me, and that's enough."

"I wouldn't be surprised if it's more than a vacation he'll be needing," Jack said. "It's a good thing he can afford the best doctors. Something like this would just about kill me."

Eric sat down, and the two men reviewed the events of the day. Jack was questioning his part in the whole thing.

"I'm kicking myself for not making sure that the road was clear for the pickup. I probably could have got Willis or Brown to do a little juggling of the schedule, to keep that patrol car away a little longer."

Eric's face showed his concern. "You can't keep beating yourself up about something that wasn't really under your control. How were you supposed to know that traffic division would choose that very moment to place an officer in that spot? Um, can you do anything to keep it from happening the next time?"

"You can be sure I'm going to try," Jack said. His spirits had lifted, if only a very little.

"Tea?" Eric asked.

"Yeah, that would do nicely just about now. I was sort of looking forward to that four-course breakfast in the morning, though."

"Dream on. I'll go try to make that kettle work."

A while later, Eric informed Jack that the tea was ready.

"I'll let you make your own and doctor it your way.

It's the least I can do, since breakfast will be such a disappointment."

Eric smiled as his friend came around the counter that divided the kitchen from the living room in the little apartment.

They took their hot drinks and a half-eaten package of cookies that Eric had managed to find back to the couch and sat down.

"So how's your love life?" Eric asked.

"That's kind of a strange question under the circumstances, don't you think? Personal too."

"I just thought that it would be good to get our minds off all that's been occupying them for so long. If you don't want to talk, that's okay, Jack. I didn't mean for you to take me too literally, by the way. I was just wondering how things are going between you and Valerie. She's quite a treasure, if you don't mind me saying so."

"Well, you can't have her," Jack said, smiling now.

"I take it that means that things are still going well between the two of you."

Jack nodded. A look of contentment was replacing the taut expression that had been a constant companion for the past few hours.

"You know, you two ought to give some consideration to making this relationship permanent. You don't want to lose her to a guy like . . ." Here he did his best to make the sound of dramatic music. "Dunh, dunh, dunh—Keegan Willis."

"Fat chance," Jack said. "She gets to see and hear him firsthand. It is not a match she is apt to make in this lifetime. I've thought about proposing, but I'm never sure when the right time would be."

"How about some evening when the two of you are having a quiet dinner together. Soon is good." Eric smiled.

"She's got a career. I've got whatever life this is. But I guess you're right. I've got to admit that I really want to spend the rest of that life with Val. I'll let you know as soon as we make any decisions. Time to change the subject."

They talked into the early morning, neither one feeling particularly tired and both fearful that they would not sleep. They decided it was a better use of time and less frustrating to share each other's company.

Herties had apparently managed either to fall asleep or immerse himself in one of the books that Eric kept in the spare room for guests.

The bedroom door was closed and light came from beneath it, but there was no sound of restlessness coming from the man inside.

Eventually, Eric excused himself and said he was going to lie down for a while. Jack was left sitting on the couch.

He turned himself sideways and propped himself up on a pillow his friend had retrieved from a hall cupboard along with a blanket. Jack turned out the light and covered himself as best he could.

His mind was still reeling with thoughts of the day just past and concerns for the day that was about to start.

Chapter Eighteen
She's Come Undone

When Jack opened his eyes again, the sun was up and the smell of freshly brewed coffee filled the air.

Over the top of the counter, he could see Eric moving about in the kitchen. He was in the midst of preparing something, but Jack could not tell what it was from where he lay.

Eric noticed him watching.

"Well, good morning. I gather you got a little rest, at least. I was able to sneak past you to do some shopping and get back without disturbing you, it seems."

"I guess I was tired after all," Jack admitted. "How about you?"

"I slept a little. Of course, I was in my own bed, so it was probably easier for me than for you or Mr. Herties."

"Is he up?" Jack asked.

"Yeah. He's in the shower. I loaned him a dressing gown. He should be out for breakfast in a moment or two."

"I thought breakfast was out of the question," Jack said, surprise evident in his voice.

"It was mostly the 'four-course' part that was causing the problem. This isn't haute cuisine, but it should tide you over until a little later."

As it turned out, Eric had visited the doughnut shop down the road and had brought back a selection of their finest wares.

"This isn't half bad," Jack said as he sat down with two of the pastries and a cup of Eric's coffee. "I hope you didn't think I was serious when I said I wanted a big breakfast."

"Jack, how many years have we known one another? Don't you think I can tell when you are serious and when you are not?"

"I'm kind of depending on my ability to lie to get us through this situation we're trying to resolve. And the answers are 'ten' and 'yes, I do.' By the way, I'm glad you think you know me that well." Jack took a bite of his doughnut and washed it down with a sip of his coffee.

Eric placed a mug and a plate across from Jack. "We'll let Mr. Herties sit here," he said as he put a paper napkin beside the place setting.

A few moments later, Wolf Herties appeared from his room looking somewhat refreshed. He had shaved, using a disposable that Eric had provided, and had managed to keep his clothes from the day before from getting too wrinkled.

There was no hiding the tension he must have been feeling. He moved with a stiffness not brought on by his sleeping accommodations. His brow bore a perpetual wrinkle. His mouth turned downward at the edges. It was clear that today would have to resolve the problems at hand, or they would break the man who could buy anything but deliverance from fear and the wicked plans of others.

"Good morning, gentlemen. And I do hope and pray that it will be a good morning," Herties said.

"I must confess, Eric, that I found my accommodations very comfortable and that, once I fell asleep, I slept well. I'm feeling physically rested. My mind is still a little overexercised. I hope I can get off that treadmill by the end of the day." He smiled at them both.

To Jack, it seemed the smile was intended to convey the message that there should not be any more missteps from his quarter. It was a look he had seen before, on the face of another multimillionaire just before he told someone for all the world to see, "You're fired."

"Mr. Herties, it is my earnest expectation that we will get your daughter to you today, alive and well," Jack said, convincingly he hoped.

Herties gave a nod and a weak smile. "Pass the doughnuts, please."

Jack passed the plate and filled the man's cup from the thermos Eric had placed in the center of the table.

They ate in silence, Herties' appetite apparently little affected by the worry Jack knew lay just below the surface.

Eric was clearing the dishes when Herties asked Jack, "What is the plan for today? When do you think we will hear from Jen?"

"I can't be sure, but I'll need to make a call very soon. We need to be ready when Jen calls. I'll explain things as we go. I hope that's all right with you. It makes it easier to follow, in case something has to be changed."

"I'll have to trust you, I guess," Herties said.

"I can tell you this," Jack said. "Once we hear from your daughter, the police will immediately be involved and will do all they can to ensure that Jennifer is safe. You will have to wait until Fretz calls with the plans for the exchange. Our next step will depend on what he says. I have plans, either way."

Herties appeared to accept the explanation and didn't ask any further questions.

The change of plans from the night before had put a kink in the arrangements Jack had been making the previous afternoon. He knew that his contact had passed the word to the next shift. At least the word Jack wanted them to hear had been passed.

He had had to tell a small lie in order to save a life. It seemed like a fair trade to make. He hoped that the folks who ruled on such things would feel the same way.

He dialed the same number he had called the previous afternoon and spoke in quiet tones to the person on the other end.

The only explanation he offered to Herties and Eric was, "It's part of a plan I've devised. If it works, we may be able to get Jennifer back before the drop. We'll have to see."

As it turned out, they did not have to wait very long before Jack could put his plan into action.

The ringing of a phone brought all three men to attention. Most shocking was which phone rang.

Herties snatched up his cell phone and snapped it open.

He placed the device to his ear and said, "Herties here. I'm afraid I'm a little busy right now, could you call . . ."

He stopped in midsentence, then, "Jennifer, where are you? How are you? Are you all right? Has he been abusing you?"

Jack whispered to Eric, "She knows his number, and it was forwarded here. That's why she's on his phone and not yours."

"Sir, it's important that we get some other questions answered," Jack said quietly, resting a hand lightly on the man's shoulder. "Ask her if she is alone."

Herties asked the question and listened to the answer. He nodded a vigorous affirmation. Covering the mouthpiece, he said, "She says she's okay. She hasn't been assaulted, but she doesn't know where she is. She says she's in some kind of a box. I can't imagine what . . ."

Jack's full attention was now on the phone.

"Sir, I hate to ask, but might I speak to her for a moment? It is very important."

Herties looked stricken, then said into the phone, "Jen, honey, I want you to speak to a friend of mine. His name is Jack. He's trying to help us get you back."

He passed his phone to Jack.

"Hi, Jennifer. I'll speak quickly, but I need some information from you."

Jack heard a soft "Okay" from the other end.

"What kind of phone do you have there?"

The response was almost whispered. "It's a cell phone. Look, he told me not to talk long. He said he'd be listening. I'm afraid."

"You say you are in some sort of enclosure."

"He put me in a big box. Said that it was too dangerous for me to stay at his place. The box was in the back of his truck. He drove me here, blindfolded. Made me get in the box. I've been here a long time. I think I slept some."

"Is he close by?" Jack asked.

"I don't know. He opened the box, dropped in the phone, and told me to call my dad. He closed the lid, and I think he's locked it. I think I heard him walking away. I'm outside somewhere."

"Okay, Jennifer. I'm going to talk. You just listen. After I've explained all this, I'm going to hang up. No matter what happens, I want you to dial 911 on that cell phone."

"But he told me not to try anything like that."

"Just do what I say. It will be all right. Dial 911 after I hang up, and just lay the phone down. Do not talk, but do not hang up. If you hear him coming, hang up and dial your father's number. That will at least clear the 911 from the screen. I doubt he'll look at the call history. Do you understand?"

"Yes. Can I talk to my dad?" the shaky voice asked.

"Just to say good-bye," Jack said firmly. "You've got to call that number right away."

He handed the phone to Herties, who told her of his love and that all would be all right, and then reluctantly handed the device back to Jack.

"Call now," he said and hung up before there could be any further protest.

Jack was now the center of attention. The two men just stared, waiting for some sort of explanation. Jack picked up the phone again and keyed in a number.

"We'll know in a few moments whether I've done you a terrible disservice or if we have found your daughter.

"Hi, Karl. It's Jack again. Got anything for me?" He listened. A look of satisfaction spread across his face.

"You're a lifesaver, Karl. Remind me. I owe you one . . . Yeah, I thought I'd just test my equipment, to see if it was working . . . I appreciate your help . . . Bye for now." He hung up.

It was Eric's turn to ask questions.

"Alright, Jack, spill the beans. What was that all about?"

Jack sat down again and pulled out his cell phone.

"This, gentlemen, is a digital cell phone. Technology has advanced since the first ones that looked like and weighed as much as a brick."

"Please come to the point, Jack," a frustrated Wolf Herties demanded.

Jack looked at his watch and appeared to make a mental calculation.

"I've only got a second or two, but Jenny confirmed what I had thought, from the way Fretz was setting up the call. He had to take her a phone—a cell phone. I suspect that if we dig around enough, we will find out that he bought a prepaid phone under an assumed name. No matter. The police will deal with that.

"Listen. Do you mind if I set the rest of this plan in motion before I finish the explanation? I've got a girl who needs rescuing."

Herties looked excited about Jack's comments but had

no time to comment. The private investigator was back on the phone again.

"Keegan, Jack Elton. Sorry to keep you in the dark. Get in touch with Karl at the fire hall. He's got a call for you to track. He thinks you and I are checking equipment, so don't tell him the real reason. I owe you one."

Jack came off the phone and, looking Herties square in the eye, reported, "Sir, I'm happy to inform you that the police will shortly be bringing your daughter back to you."

"What's going on?" the father asked.

"Digital phones have advanced, along with the rest of telephone technology. These days, when you call the emergency number from a home phone, your address flashes on the screen. Even if you hang up beforehand, your details will be available for police, fire, and ambulance.

"Until recently, if you used a cell phone you'd have to be able to tell them where you were. It was a real beast if you either didn't know or weren't able to speak. Fortunately for us, that all changed after 9/11 when the phone companies started adding the technology that allowed phones to be located by GPS. Their intention wasn't to track people in trouble, initially. They wanted to be able to locate terrorists. But there was the added bonus of now being able to locate folks making 911 calls."

"And that means?" Herties asked impatiently.

"That means that a satellite way up there," Jack pointed to the ceiling, "can figure out, to within about a hundred yards, where you are calling from and send that information to the boys and girls in the emergency response radio room."

"So where is Jennifer?" Herties asked.

"I don't know. I didn't ask for too many details from Karl. He's on dispatch this morning. I told him we were testing phone equipment. I didn't want to have him raising too many alarms just yet.

"He did mention a general location. It was not Fretz's neighborhood. I suspect it will be somewhere away from too much regular traffic."

"Shouldn't you be going to get her?" Eric asked, indicating the other two.

"I don't think so," Jack said, holding up a hand of caution. "The police need to go looking for Jennifer in their car. They have to depend on information relayed to them over their police radio. It may take a while to pinpoint the exact location, and Keegan Willis may have to wade through some mud and wet grass to get to her." He smiled.

"I bet you're hoping he does, Jack," Eric said with a knowing wink.

"It will do him good to have to exercise a little, but I'm praying that he finds the box quickly."

"The box?" Eric asked. A look of surprise mixed with fear covered his face.

"Fretz built a box to put Jennifer in, in case he needed to hide her," Jack said. "When the report about her disappearance was broadcast on the news, he had to use it. He may have been planning to bury her if things got really tense.

"The fact that he gave her the opportunity to talk to you tells me that he thought better of that plan. I believe the box will be found aboveground, but probably not out in the open. He'd have to wrestle the thing into position himself. It won't be too far from a place where he can safely stop his truck. We should know soon enough."

"What a dunce," Eric said.

"Maybe," said Jack, "but I think he has a soft spot for you, Mr. Herties, in spite of what he says. I doubt he would have caused your daughter any real harm."

"That is yet to be seen," Herties said. His anger flared against his daughter's kidnapper. "If he wanted to show me how much of a soft spot he had, he would have left well enough alone. Any soft spot he might have is in his head, by my estimation," the millionaire said. "What do we do now?"

"I'm going to need your help and a little patience," Jack answered. "I realize that this is difficult for you, but it should start to resolve itself rather quickly now. I'm sorry to tell you we need to wait. There should be a phone call soon that will make you feel better."

Herties nodded in resignation. He rose from his seat and went to the bedroom.

He returned a short while later with his coat over one arm and the briefcase in the other hand. He deposited the coat on a chair and placed the money beside it.

It was a half hour before Jack's cell phone began to ring. He looked at his watch. It was almost nine.

He snapped the phone open. "Jack here," he said.

"It's Keegan here. We've tracked the phone call. You'll never guess where that box has been—all night, I would assume."

"How about you tell me, detective?" Jack said.

"There's a hiking trail that cuts through the area—a former railroad right of way. The box was off the path a little ways in a gulley, so it couldn't be seen from the trail."

"How's the girl? Where's our culprit?" Jack asked.

"Sorry, Jack. We've got an empty."

Chapter Nineteen
Here We Go Again

Keegan Willis sounded like a man who had been beaten.

"Guy's nowhere around. We've got the box, a few tire tracks, and that's it. It looks like our man has other plans."

Jack covered the phone and turned to an anxious-looking Wolf Herties.

"I'm afraid it's not over yet, sir. I'm sorry," he said.

Pain was immediately on the father's face.

"What's that?" Jack heard Willis ask over the phone.

"Sorry, Keegan, just informing Mr. Herties that he'll have to wait a little longer to see his daughter. He will see her eventually, though, won't he?"

"I think so, Jack. There's no sign of any violence. Not here, at least. He built the thing to make her as comfortable as possible. Put air holes in it but was careful not to put any where she could see out. We seem to have two sets of footprints. Some sort of hiking boot and a set of running shoes. Small. The girl walked, or was led, to the box to get in. Looks like she got out. Both sets lead to where the truck was parked. Then again, you never know. Don't tell the dad I said that."

"Okay. Tell me about these other plans you think he has," Jack said.

"He'll probably call Dad and make plans for a drop. Then he'll either tell you where to find her or have you wait while he sets her free to find her own way out."

"I'm assuming you don't know where he has gone. Thanks for trying, anyway. I guess we'll just have to wait for his next move," Jack said.

"That would be best. Pretend we never had this conversation."

"What conversation?" Jack replied.

"Gotta go. Got police work to do here. Call downtown later. I'll let you know if we turn anything up."

Jack hung up and took a few moments to compose himself. Then he tried to explain what Keegan Willis had said. He was careful not to extinguish the last embers of hope for Jennifer's quick recovery.

"I'm sure that they will be on the lookout for Fretz's truck and will probably want to tail him once they catch up with him. But I'm going to try to cover a few more bases."

Jack called Valerie, who was overcome at the news that the girl had not been found.

"You probably know that this isn't the end of it," Valerie reminded him. "I'm guessing that they want to make the collar stick so they are planning on letting you go through with the drop.

"Be careful, Jack," she said. "The girl's not safe, and

you know it now. Don't let your guard down for a moment. I don't want you to get into any trouble you can't get out of."

"I'll be sure of that. And one more thing . . ." Jack said.

"What's that?"

"Could you check with traffic and see if there are any speed traps scheduled for out this way? I'd appreciate a heads-up this time. They might want to confer with Willis on that too. I'm sure he doesn't want his big bust getting away on him."

"I'll get on that right away, Jack. Take care. Call me tonight—early if possible."

"Roger and out," Jack said, closing his cell phone and returning to the living room couch.

Eric's phone had not rung yet, but all three men were anticipating that it would not be much longer. Jack suspected that Fretz wasn't too terribly original. If his assessment was right, the instructions and timing would be similar to those of the previous failed attempt. He wondered, though, if he might have underestimated the man prematurely.

They sat and talked. The mood was much less relaxed than before. Now they needed not only to follow the directions that they hoped would shortly come, but also to be able to pull off whatever manipulation was necessary so that the police could finally complete their work.

The call came at quarter to eleven. Wolf Herties took a deep breath as Eric answered the phone.

He listened and nodded as the caller spoke, giving grunts

of affirmation in response to each instruction. He made notes on a pad as Jack watched over his shoulder.

"Look, I didn't call them yesterday. I didn't call them today. That was just a coincidence. I want my daughter back. That's my only concern. You'll get your money . . . yes. Good-bye."

He hung up.

Jack had been reading the notes as the conversation progressed.

"Doesn't digress from the original by much, does it?" he said.

"I suppose not," Herties agreed, looking up from Eric's notes.

"Alright, Eric, we're on the road again," Jack said. "I see that this time we're off to the shopping center by the parkway. I'll let you know how things go."

Jack turned to Wolf Herties, who was by now looking completely on the alert. "Let's go, sir. It's a little further away. We don't want to be late for our appointment."

Herties was on his feet, coat and case in hand, and standing by the door.

"The sooner we get this done, the sooner I can see my girl," he said. "Thank you for your hospitality, Eric. You've been a wonderful host. I hope to have the opportunity to pay you back sometime soon."

"It was a pleasure to have you," Eric replied. "It was no trouble at all. Good luck today, sir."

They shook hands all around, and Jack left with his passenger.

The two men drove along the road and turned up to the

parkway that would lead them to the shopping mall. As they went, Jack thought he heard the man beside him humming quietly. All was about to be well with the world again for Wolf Herties, at least as long as nothing happened to foil the plan.

At the shopping center, Jack pulled into a parking spot near the entrance. Because of the way the lot was laid out and the location of the phones, Herties would have to walk a short distance to the main doors and wait by the bank of booths inside. A clock over the information kiosk would indicate when the call was about to come.

Just as it had the day before, the phone began to ring at the agreed-upon time. When it did, Herties noted the directions and hurried back to the car.

"The golf course," he said as he slipped into the backseat.

"What?" Jack asked.

"The golf course south of here. Continue down the parkway."

"Then what?" Jack asked, setting the car in motion and driving to the exit.

"On the way back from the clubhouse, there is a short road to the right. It leads to the driving range. I'm supposed to leave the money in a trash bin at the junction of the two. We drive out the rest of the way and head west to the next road. It's a close. We drive to the end and wait."

"I think he's made things a little easier for our friends, who will want to have a little chat with him after all this. Lots of cars up there. Lots of people. He'll go unnoticed by most, except the folks who know he'll be rummaging in the trash."

Jack pulled out his phone and called the police

headquarters. He asked to speak with Detective Willis. Once he was connected, he explained what was planned.

"If you send an unmarked car up there, you can park and look just like the rest of the folks. Just keep an eye on the garbage can. We're still on our way up. Should be there in about ten minutes."

Jack drove to the golf course and turned up the long drive to the clubhouse. At the parking lot, he drove through to the exit and started back down the drive. The road to the driving range was now to his right. The trash can was a few feet from the intersection. There were a number of empty cars parked along the roadway. No one seemed to notice when Herties slipped out of the backseat and dropped the briefcase into the receptacle. If Keegan's man was there, he was doing a good job of keeping out of sight.

They followed the instructions Herties had been given and drove to the traffic circle at the end of the close.

And they waited.

The sound of screaming sirens, accompanied by the roar of high-powered engines, brought a chill to Jack's heart.

Chapter Twenty
The End of the Road . . . Almost

As he looked toward the end of the street, he could briefly see the bright red and blue of the light bars as two patrol cars pursued an old pickup that rocketed along the intersecting road.

Wolf Herties heard and saw the police chase too. He had moved into the passenger seat beside Jack as soon as they had arrived at the location where Fretz had told them to wait. He now leaned forward and looked at Jack, eyebrows raised and shrugged, palms upraised.

"Is that about us?" he asked.

"I don't think so," Jack replied. "I'm quite sure that wasn't Fretz's truck they were chasing. His is much newer."

"Do you think they have Jen?"

"Dunno," Jack said. "In any case, they seem too occupied right now to call us with any news. I guess we just have to sit tight."

"Here?" Herties asked.

"Here is as good as anyplace else. Let's just stick to our plan. We may need to go somewhere with the police."

"If we don't hear back after a while, maybe we can go back to Eric's," Herties suggested. "You don't think he would mind?"

"He's willing to do whatever is necessary in order to bring this all to a successful conclusion, sir." Jack rolled down his window and stuck his elbow out the opening. *We could be here for a while yet,* he thought.

It was almost an hour before Jack's phone rang. Keegan Willis said, simply, "We got him, Jack. Unfortunately, we don't have the girl. But we have the money. And Jack . . ."

"Yeah," Jack said, a feeling of dread rising within himself.

"He's not talking. Says he wants to have a little chat with Wolf Herties."

"What about?" Jack asked.

"Says he wants to make a deal. Maybe you ought to bring Daddy along to the station so we can get this sorted out as quickly as possible. I'll call ahead and arrange for an interview room. We'll get our suspect booked and then see what he has to offer."

"Okay, we'll meet you there," Jack said. He started the car and pulled away for the drive back into the city.

"What's going on?" Herties asked, looking up suddenly. He had been dozing when Jack's phone rang.

"We're going to get your daughter back, but it looks like you're going to need your negotiating skills. Fretz wants to deal."

"You mean Jen hasn't been found? What is happening? What has he done . . ."

"Sir, I think it is all going to work out. I don't want to alarm you, but we need to work quickly. If Bernard Fretz is working alone, as I suspect, he may have put her back in that box, and we don't know where it is this time. I'm certain he didn't leave any means of locating her, either. I know I'm being a little blunt, but this guy isn't thinking straight and he may get Jen into more trouble than he realizes, if he leaves her in a location that is unsafe. Your money is safe. Now let's go and talk to Fretz, shall we?"

"Thanks, Jack. I really do appreciate all that you've done. But the money is insignificant compared to having Jen back."

"We'll need your assistance, sir, in getting this man to justice. I hope you won't mind cooperating with the police in that regard."

"It will be my distinct pleasure," the man replied with a faint smile.

The two men drove toward town without speaking, except to make the occasional observation about traffic. From time to time Herties would sigh deeply.

When he looked over at Jennifer's father, Jack could see that the man was deeply troubled.

"Jack, I've been thinking," Herties said suddenly, breaking the silence. "I think I know what he wants."

"What do you mean?" Jack asked, genuinely curious about the older man's words.

"Well," the father replied, "Fretz has been arrested. And I'm sure he deserves to be punished for what he did to Jen.

He deserves to be punished for the emotional pain Jen and I have had to endure as well. If he's hurt her in any way, I'd likely try to kill him with my own bare hands."

"Sir, the police will deal with all that. Mr. Fretz will be duly tried, sentenced, and imprisoned. Your daughter is going to be just fine. And . . ."

"I'm not through," Herties interrupted. "It's why he did it that concerns me."

"He did it to hurt you," Jack said as he maneuvered the car through the downtown traffic.

"Okay, Jack, he did it to hurt me because he believed I hurt him unjustly. I'm not saying that he wasn't wrong. But I think I owe it to him to be certain I had a valid reason to fire him in the first place."

"So, what do you think he wants?"

"I want Schreiver to confess. I want you to admit you were wrong. I want my job back."

Bernard Fretz sat across the interview table from Wolf Herties and Jack Elton. He was shackled hand and foot and desperately needed a shave and a shower, too, from the assault his presence was making on Jack's olfactory nerves.

Two uniformed officers stood by the door. Keegan Willis sat next to the prisoner.

Fretz had been processed after his arrest and was facing, among other things, charges of kidnapping and extortion. It was yet to be determined if other charges might be brought. It all depended on how this interview went and Jennifer Herties' physical state when, and if, she was found.

"Mr. Fretz, it seems to me you are hardly in a position to be demanding anything at this point," Willis said, affecting his tough cop persona and apparently forgetting for the moment that the prisoner was in a bargaining position, unless there was an immanent break in the investigation.

"May I speak?" Wolf Herties asked, addressing himself to the detective.

Willis nodded his assent.

"Bernie, I need to know that Jen is safe. You're in a lot of trouble right now and I don't think either you or I want things to get any worse. Can you assure me that my daughter is okay?"

"Safe enough for now," Fretz replied. "Maybe not too safe if this thing drags on, if you get my drift. Get me what I want. Promise to give me my job back once I get out of this mess, and I'll tell this nice man," he nodded toward Willis, "where to find her. I don't suppose you're going to be on the hook for the job anytime soon, but I need something to look forward to. And I need to be vindicated as far as the embezzling accusations are concerned. If I were you, I'd start looking for Schreiver right away."

"What about Jen's safety in the meantime?" Jack asked.

"You're the guy who came to the house the other day, aren't you? Let me just say that everything I told you that day is the absolute truth. It's what's making me crazy. It's what's got me into this fix. As far as Jen is concerned, well, let me just say that she has food and water. Not a lot. She's secure and out of the weather. That's all you get for now. Do we have a deal, Mr. Big Bad Wolf?"

Chapter Twenty-one
Back on the Road Again

Valerie was almost in tears, and Jack didn't know why. Was it the sad story of Jennifer Herties, who was still missing? Maybe it was the news of his impending trip that was causing the waterworks. He was afraid to ask, lest he look like an idiot or be judged insensitive.

Relationships can be so confusing, he thought. He decided to wait it out and see whether Valerie would give some clue to why she was being so emotional. He didn't have to wait long.

"Do you mean to say that old man Herties is planning on sending you away to track down this guy Schreiver? He still has his money. I'm sure the police have the resources to track down his daughter. She can't be far away now. Why is he sending you? What else does he need?"

"Well, he would like to see his daughter alive—and soon," Jack said.

"He's not satisfied with the legal system? Can't the police handle this? What else could he possibly accomplish by sending you on some wild goose chase south of the border?"

"It's not a wild goose chase if it results in Jen finally coming home. I guess he trusts me. I've apparently made some sort of impression on the old guy. But that's not really what's making you sad and angry, is it?" Jack asked.

Valerie Cummins burst into tears. All Jack could think to do was envelop her in his arms and hold on until she calmed down. It seemed to work.

She stopped crying and looked up into his face, her eyes red and her cheeks wet with tears.

"I know it sounds foolish. I shouldn't have said those things. I'm being selfish, I guess. I don't want you to go. I'd worry about you all the time you were gone," she said and wiped her eyes with the back of her hand.

"Help me out here," Jack said. "Is that a good thing or a bad thing?"

"You silly man," Valerie said. "I love you and can't stand to be without you. You decide."

"Okay, let's see. It's umm . . . Wow, that's a toughie. You can't help me out, eh?"

"Here it is, Jack. Pay attention. I don't want you to go away, because I cannot bear to be away from you. So your trip for Herties will be a bad thing, for me, at any rate. On the other hand, I think it's good that you have the respect of the richest man in the city, maybe the richest man in the country. And that's kind of good. And I know you'll succeed. Jen Herties will soon be home safe and sound. You've got to decide whether my loving you so much that it hurts is good or bad."

"I think I've made up my mind already. I mean, I think I've made up my mind about a lot of things. I promise I'll make it all up to you when I get back. But for right now, I don't even know for sure where Wolf Herties wants me to go. Don't know that even he knows."

"What exactly did he say?" Valerie asked.

"Let's sit down," Jack said. "The coffee looks ready. I'll pour."

The two of them retreated to Valerie's living room, where they sat together on her couch.

Jack had come to the apartment after he had received instructions from Herties indicating that he wanted the private eye to be the one to find Ben Schreiver who, it appeared now, had been the real culprit and had diverted attention from himself to the man whose actions he was supposed to be investigating.

He had told Jack he wasn't exactly sure of the schedule yet but would get back to him soon. Keegan Willis had been convinced and in turn had advised Detective Sergeant Ted Brown that Herties had connections that would help speed up the process. The detectives had given Jack thirty-six hours to make his inquiries. In the meantime, they would do their own sleuthing in the city to try to track down the kidnapped girl.

Willis had made sure that Fretz was aware that if the girl was found before Jack got back, all bets were off and the full force of the law would fall on him at once.

Herties had said he was making inquiries with some of his friends down south. Jack did not want to ask who they might be.

"The old man, as you call him, thinks Fretz is telling the truth, at least as far as his innocence in the company theft is concerned. Schreiver was higher in the system when the money went missing. Herties thought he was trustworthy. Suddenly it appears that cash is missing. Schreiver hears about Herties' suspicions and comes to him and suggests that someone is dipping into the pot, so to speak. He lets it drop that maybe Fretz is the guilty party. Neat ploy if, as W. D. suspects, it's Schreiver who is the guilty party."

"So it's a set-up job, and Fretz is the guy who's taking the fall?" Valerie asked.

"That is the prevailing theory," Jack said. "Herties believed the snitch and, because of his seniority, Schreiver gets put in charge of the investigation. And no, you don't have to tell me what a bad move that was, regardless of who was taking the cash. So Fretz gets fired. I gather he was not granted the courtesy of any sort of appeal. Schreiver made sure his report implicated the guy. Herties tells me it was quite a document, and very convincing."

"So Fretz gets fired . . ."

"And Schreiver gets away," Jack added. "And now W. D. wants to find this guy. Fretz wants him found so that he can be exonerated. Mind you, he's got worse problems now than he ever thought he had before. What he's planning on doing if, and when, Schreiver surfaces, is a mystery to me at the moment. And if we can't prove Schreiver is the real guilty party, I don't know what happens to Jen. You can understand that I'm feeling driven to get this situation resolved."

"I know you have to do this, Jack. I'm just being selfish, I guess. I wish someone else could go instead of you. It's a long way to go to track a guy who probably doesn't want to be found."

"But I'll be back," Jack said.

"Yeah, but you'll be gone first."

"I said I'd make it up to you. And I will," Jack assured her.

"Okay, let's assume you find Schreiver. What next?"

"I don't know. I think Fretz thinks he'll confess to the whole thing. He'll probably figure he's safe. And he probably would have been, had it not been for Fretz doing the dumb thing that he did. That made Herties mad. Money he can replace, but touch his one and only daughter and he wants revenge. Strangely, he understands why Fretz did what he did. But he's mad—really mad—at the guy that made him do it. Money like W. D. has can buy some pretty long arms to get back at a guy like Schreiver. I'm just glad all I've got to do is find him. It's just like when I was serving papers on people. I only had to let them know they were in trouble. Someone else made sure they had their day in court."

"I don't want you to go," Valerie said.

"I know. But I will be back. I promise."

Jack wanted to give further assurance that he would be all right and that the trip away would not be a long one. He didn't get the chance.

They had not finished their coffee or their conversation before Jack's cell phone began to ring. It was W. D. Herties, and he wanted to see Jack right away.

"Jack, I'm sending you to a nice warm place for a while," Herties said after the private investigator had settled into one of the leather chairs in the millionaire's office.

I'm feeling like I'm already in a very warm place, Jack thought as he reflected on the pain he had felt at having to leave Valerie in the state she had been.

"You're going to California to talk to Ben Schreiver for me and for Fretz, but especially for Jen," Herties continued. "I doubt that there is much we can do to him, at this point. He probably won't want to cooperate with you, but I've got to give it a try. I've got to get my daughter back."

"We don't even know where Schreiver is," Jack said. "I'm not so sure this deal you've made is the best move."

"I've got some leads for you to follow," Herties said. "All I want you to do is try and find this man and get any evidence you can that will make him confess. Knowing that he knows I'm aware of his deceit will be some compensation. But I won't rest until I have Jen back home. Time is tight. Don't let me down."

"I'll do my best, sir. No guarantees, you understand."

"I understand." Herties looked grim.

"Now, who do I contact when I get to California?" Jack asked.

"Here are your ticket and a list," the millionaire replied.

Chapter Twenty-two
I Left My Heart . . . Somewhere

"I'll never complain about traffic back home ever again," Jack said to himself as he fought himself along the Los Angeles freeway.

He was heading toward Palm Springs, and the going was painfully slow. Unfortunately, he had arrived at LAX early enough in the day to be right in the midst of rush hour.

That's the oxymoron of the century, he thought. Rush-hour traffic, especially here, was anything but rushing.

Eventually, Jack made his way closer to the resort town. He was fascinated by the windmill farms on the side of the hills in the San Gorgonio Pass, outside Palm Springs.

Forests of modern wind-power generators provide electricity for a community with a ravenous hunger for that resource.

His destination was a little restaurant in the center of

town. He remembered that the place was famous for its food, particularly its Italian fare. He seemed to recall that it had once been owned by Sonny Bono, who had died in a tragic skiing accident some years before. Jack was old enough to remember when Sonny and Cher were topping the music charts.

Jack's appointment was with Vincent Apa, a local businessman who had made it his vocation to buy up old buildings, renovate them, and sell them for many times more than they had been worth. He was a man who took pride in what he did and was noted for being fair and honest in all his dealings. His business had become fabulously successful because of that.

Tradesmen knew that if they were contracted to work for V. A. Enterprises, they would be well paid, and the checks would always arrive on time. In return, they were expected to provide a fair day's labor and the best quality workmanship that they could muster.

It was a process that worked well for all concerned. Vincent Apa's fame had caught the attention of Wolf Herties. The two men shared business plans and strategies across the border to the benefit of both.

Apa knew Ben Schreiver. The man had done some accounting for him on Herties recommendation. Wolf had had to apologize to Vincent. When he had called to try to track down the former accountant, he discovered that Schreiver had absconded with a particularly large payroll at one of V. A. Enterprises' larger projects. This had convinced the millionaire once and for all that the man he had thought he could trust had manipulated the situation with Fretz.

"One day he was there, doing my books. The next, all that's left is a few crumpled notes in his wastebasket and an empty deposit bag," Apa said.

"You paid for contractors in cash?" Jack asked.

"Well, no. You see, I collect rents at some of my projects just before payday. The cash and checks go to the bank. And we cut checks for my contractors. I used to do it all myself, but for better or for worse, the whole thing got too big," Apa explained.

"So you gave Schreiver clearance to do your banking."

"Yeah. And he had the checkbook too. Managed to cash a big one, made out to himself, and also held back all the rents that had been paid in cash. I know it's not the way to do business. I've built up a trust with my clients. Sometimes it's easier for them to pay cash than to go through the hassle of making a check."

Jack raised his eyebrows at this, and Vincent Apa apparently saw it.

"I know what you're thinking. I want you to know that I declared all my income and paid all the taxes that needed paying. My customers know I don't take kindly to any sort of underhanded business practice."

"Wolf Herties told me about your reputation before he would even let me out of his office. I'm just surprised by your trusting nature," Jack said.

"Believe me," the real estate tycoon said, "it has gotten me into some interesting situations with less scrupulous people. But the benefits of good business practice far outweigh the disadvantages. But enough about my business. You want to know about Schreiver."

"Anything you have would be helpful," Jack said.

"Well, after he robbed me, he disappeared, like I said. I never heard from him again. I sent people looking, but he always seemed one step ahead of them. I gave up chasing after the guy."

"So you don't know where he is?" Jack asked.

"I know where he was. After he left I heard he was in Los Angeles for a while. He had some sort of advertising scam. Sold ads in a nonexistent community directory. Caught a lot of people and made some good money with that one, I hear. But when folks caught on, he vanished into the night."

"And that's all you know?" Jack asked.

"Pretty much. Oh, I've heard rumors about him showing up here and there. But nothing I could confirm. I still get big guys showing up at the office looking for him, 'cause he hasn't paid his phone bill, or mortgage, or car lease. I guess he's still using my address as his place of employment. I'm famous or something, because no one bothers to call and check until it's too late. You might want to visit the collection agencies. You might get a lead on where he has been. Sorry I can't be of more help."

"That's all right," Jack said. "I'm getting a picture of this guy and an idea of how he works. I used to be a process server. I've met him in a hundred other guys. It's been nice talking to you."

"Don't rush off," Vincent Apa said and motioned to a waiter who had been hovering behind a potted palm for some time. "Stay and have lunch with me. You should get something for your efforts. And you may need the energy."

Jack agreed, but said he couldn't stay long. The pressure of time weighed heavily.

Vincent Apa ordered, and the two men enjoyed a hurried lunch amidst the noisy crowd at the popular eatery. The subject of Ben Schreiver did not come up again until they were ready to part.

"I hope you and W. D. get some satisfaction at last," Apa said. "I'd sure be pleased to see that thief get what's coming to him."

"Well sir, I intend to do my best to find out where he is. I don't know if I can do much about getting justice. I guess it's up to the authorities here to decide what happens to him."

Jack thanked his host and headed back to his rented car. W. D. Herties had urged him to take advantage of an unlimited expense account. Jack was traveling in luxury on this trip.

Herties had given him a company credit card and had said he shouldn't be concerned about the cost during this expedition.

"Don't spare the expense and end up with some old heap that strands you on the freeway," he had said. "I need you back here soon. I want Jen back right away."

He had rejected thoughts of selecting a big town car. Instead, Jack had selected a Mercedes C-230, a vehicle that Hertz classified as a luxury sports car. It wasn't particularly sporty-looking by Jack's estimation, but he was inside the vehicle, and that was where it mattered.

One of Vincent Apa's comments had started an idea brewing in Jack's brain. Herties had quite a list of contacts but had left it to his private investigator how he dealt with it.

For his part, Jack was anxious for this whole affair to be

concluded. Anything that would shorten the time spent away from Val would be a bonus, he figured.

He called information and jotted down a couple of addresses before heading out of the parking lot.

At his first stop, a young woman with bad eyes but a good tan stared myopically at a computer screen and declared, "No sir, we've got no records for that name. You could try over the other side of the city. They're bigger. Cover the whole country. You might get a lead there."

She jotted down an address and handed it to Jack. It was a duplicate of the one he had already received from the operator.

He drove with the music loud and the windows open. The car had air-conditioning, but Jack had not felt warm for a while now.

It's good to find a place where the sun has the decency to shine in the fall, he thought as he reflected on the autumn rains back home. *I hope this is all over soon,* he reminded himself.

The office, in the center of a business complex, was bustling with activity. If he had not been aware of the fact before, Jack came to the realization quite quickly that there were an awful lot of folks who were not paying their bills.

Some of the agents were speaking conspiratorially on their phones to people who had only recently defaulted on an expected payment. Through the glass on one office door, Jack could see someone pacing, receiver to ear, and apparently laying down the law to someone who had been contacted a number of times before.

He couldn't hear what was being said, but Jack knew

from bitter experience what was being intimated to the individual on the other end of the line. There are laws against contracting for something and then not paying the bill.

"May I help you, sir?"

The voice belonged to a slender, blond sun-worshipper with pink fluorescent lipstick and a welcoming smile.

Obviously not one of the ones doing the dirty work here, Jack thought.

He presented his case, Wolf Herties' business card, and the request that he might know whether one Ben Schreiver had ever been a subject of interest to the collections agency.

"Let me take you to Mr. Mansfield. He's in charge. Perhaps he can help."

The girl led Jack between the rows of desks to an office in the back corner of the building. She knocked gently, opened the door, and introduced Jack to a tall, muscular-looking man.

"Chuck, this is Mr. Elton. He's looking for some information. I told him you were the only one who might be able to help," the girl said. She handed the man the card that Wolf Herties had assured Jack would open a few doors.

"Thanks, Brenda," Charles Mansfield said and thrust out a meaty hand in welcome. "Mr. Elton, is it? How can I help you? Please, take a seat."

He motioned with his hand and smiled a winning smile.

Step into my parlor, said the spider . . . Jack thought as he settled into the chair across from the manager's desk. He was sure that, had he been a person of interest to the company, the conversation might have turned quickly to what might legally be done to those who failed to meet their financial obligations. Mansfield would have remained standing in order to have the position of superiority, and would have moved alternately from threatening to mediating until, as they say, "there was a happy resolution to your little problem."

Chuck Mansfield sat down.

"Well, sir," Jack began.

"Call me Chuck."

The broad, well-practiced grin spread across Mansfield's face.

Crooked smile. Straight teeth, Jack thought.

Without revealing too much of the dilemma that Wolf Herties and his daughter found themselves in at present, Jack asked if he might know if Ben Schreiver's name appeared anywhere in the records of the company.

"Mr. Herties is rather anxious to know the whereabouts of this man. It's a rather pressing matter. I hope you can help. I know Mr. Herties would be grateful," Jack said.

"I only know W. D. Herties by reputation," Mansfield said. "I'm sure if it's a big enough matter for him to send you here, that we should be able to accommodate you somewhat. Of course, I can't give you details of any of Mr. Schreiver's personal matters, assuming we have anything. But I might be able to help you track down his last known residence, or where he was when he got into a situation where we would be interested in him."

"Anything you could do would be an immense help," Jack replied.

"Let's see what we can do," Mansfield said. He pulled a keyboard drawer out from under the desktop, looked at the note he had made of Schreiver's name, and typed it into the computer. He watched his screen and began to hit the scroll button.

It seemed to Jack that this process went on for a long time. He looked at his watch.

Mansfield saw him.

"A lot of folks with that name. I want to make sure we get this right the first time. I'm cross-referencing with the information you gave me about his residence in Canada. That should narrow things considerably."

Jack waited. In spite of the air-conditioning, he was beginning to feel his temperature rise.

The search continued.

"Ah, here we go," Mansfield said finally. "I think we've got your man. And look at that. I can tell you exactly where to find him. I hope you're a good talker. My experience has been that you'll need some negotiating skills to get him talking to you."

Mansfield made a note. He drew a map for the visitor from out of town and handed the paper to Jack.

"Well, look at that," Jack said. "I know where that is. Lot of famous people there. Thanks for this."

Jack left the office and smiled at Brenda, who was back at her station in reception, as he went by.

At least the directions he had would take him back toward Los Angeles. If all went well, he could still catch a plane back home that night. Hopefully, Jennifer Herties was not in any immediate peril.

He had to make a call.

Jack hoped that past friendships still counted for something. He pulled off the road and dialed directory assistance. He jotted down a number and then entered the digits. He was pleased when his call was answered quickly. An appointment was arranged.

Chapter Twenty-three
The Truth Will Set Her Free

"I guess I'm ready to talk about that thing with Herties. I don't expect that any harm will come of it now."

Ben Schreiver sat relaxed in a metal chair across the desk from Jack. He fidgeted as he spoke and cast his eyes around the little office.

Jack had learned from his friend at the oldest operating jail facility in Los Angeles County that Wolf Herties' former trusted advisor had been caught at his favorite pastime and was now resident in the Pitchess Detention Center, East Facility.

After making his phone call, he had been able to relax somewhat. His quarry was still at his last known address.

It wasn't the notorious North Facility where, just a year earlier, one prisoner had died when four thousand prisoners rioted. But Jack could tell from the number of guards watching their prisoners from various vantage points, that it was secure enough for a medium-security jail.

Jack now felt assured that Schreiver might be willing to talk. He also had the assurance that he would be well protected during this part of his quest.

"Tell me what happened," Jack said.

"There's nothing to tell, really. And I'm not so sure that I should be telling you anyway," the man said, shifting position again. "I was working for the old man, taking care of some of his finances. I was, I guess you might say, a department manager. On top of that, each of us had a portion of the receivables that we were supposed to handle."

"What led to the problem that got Fretz fired?" Jack asked, hoping that Schreiver would get to the point sooner or later. He was conscious of the fact that Jennifer still had not been found. If she was back in the coffinlike box that Fretz had built, it was imperative that there be some resolution before nightfall.

Jack was regretting the extra time spent with Vincent Apa over lunch. He had been hungry, but the meal conversation had not yielded anything new.

"You might as well know, I was fed up," Schreiver said. "Here I was, handling all this money. I could see how rich Wolf Herties was getting at my expense. I figured he would hardly miss a few hundred thousand spread out over a number of months."

"You were wrong," Jack said, knowing the man across from him was well aware of the fact.

"Yeah, I was wrong. I figured that was the end of it for me. Believe me. I was as shocked as Fretz was when I suggested to Herties that he was taking the money, and the old guy believed it."

"But you helped engineer that," Jack said.

"Well, yeah. The old man comes to me all secretive and everything and says he thinks someone is dipping into the funds. We talked about possible suspects."

"You made sure he didn't put you on the list," Jack said.

"That goes without saying. Anyway, W. D. looks over the field of candidates and asks me to check up on Fretz. A few well-chosen words, some intimations of impropriety, and he's convinced Fretz is his man. I didn't dissuade him from that opinion. The rest is history."

"So, you're saying it was never Bernard Fretz who had a hand in the proverbial till?" Jack asked.

"I figure I got nothing to lose by confessing that," Schreiver said.

The man was talking as though he figured he was beyond the reach of Canadian law. Jack suspected that with some of the contacts Herties had, that was not strictly the case. He kept his suspicions to himself.

"Would you be willing to write a letter to Mr. Herties to that effect, right now?" Jack asked. "Like I told you, when I first got here, Fretz has taken matters into his own hands and is demanding to be exonerated. You're down here now. And he's had to pay the price for your crime. Jennifer Herties may be in grave danger, if you won't help us out. Consider it an opportunity to redeem yourself. Who knows how it might be a valuable bargaining tool at some point in your future?"

Schreiver's eyes darted around the office again. He shifted uneasily, scratching his chin as if considering his options.

The guards, Jack knew, were seeing and hearing what their guest was saying. He marveled at the self-control that enabled them to look as if they were unaware of what was going on before them.

"Yeah, I guess so," Schreiver said, having apparently made up his mind. "Got a pen?" he asked and looked around the room again. "I hope you'll tell Herties that I'm sorry. I figure I won't be seeing him in the near future."

A while later, the document was completed. It was a signed confession, duly witnessed, and contained specific details that Fretz had made part of his demand before he would be willing to reveal Jennifer Herties' location.

As Jack left Schreiver, he said, "I guess I should thank you, on behalf of Fretz and the Herties family. You may hear from me again."

"Trust me, friend," Schreiver said. "I won't be leaving town anytime soon. I got plenty of reason to stay right here in beautiful California."

"I guess you do," Jack said, surveying Schreiver's place of residence. And then he left for his journey home as quickly as he could.

He drove back to LAX and returned his rented Mercedes. He wished it were his own.

At least I have had a small taste of luxury, he thought as he dropped the keys in the quick-returns slot.

Inside the terminal, he checked in for his flight and found the nearest pay phone.

First he called Wolf Herties to let him know the trip had ended successfully. Then he called Ted Brown at police headquarters.

"Ted, pass on to Fretz that he's got what he wanted, in spades. Assure him that he will see the confession as soon as I can get back. Try to get him to talk about where he has hidden the girl. I'm sure Dad would be glad to have her back."

"Thanks, Jack. I'll do that right away. I'll let him know the trouble any stalling could cause him. You'll have to see him in the morning, though. By the time you get back, we'll be all locked down for the night. Fretz will be all tucked in and warm, at taxpayers' expense."

Talk to ya when I get back," Jack said and hung up the phone.

Just then, he heard the first call for his flight home. He was looking forward to the return trip. Valerie was back there. Jennifer Herties would soon be heading home. Hopefully, Wolf Herties would be thankful in a material way. And Jack had a first-class ticket for the trip back to all of that.

It was late that evening when Jack's flight arrived at the Vancouver airport. The trip had been uneventful and, in fact, he had been able to doze for a while after finishing his airline dinner.

The food was never as bad as many people suggested, and certainly more plentiful than the fare that was served in coach class. He wondered, though, whether having a job that forced him to eat most of his meals aboard a flying metal tube might cause him to rethink that opinion.

He had left his car in the Park 'n' Fly lot, so he waited at the shuttle stop for the bus that would take him between the rows of vehicles to section 4A. The car would be cold and not nearly as comfortable as the set of wheels he had been forced to part with at LAX. He was always impressed by the difference in temperature represented by the scant few degrees of latitude between California and British Columbia.

He drove home in the dark and parked outside the front door of the building that housed both his office and his apartment.

Too late to call Val tonight, he thought as he climbed the stairs past the second floor. He did not even glance toward his office as he ascended to the third floor. *Plenty of time for office matters tomorrow. Maybe the day after tomorrow.*

Jack unlocked his door and walked into the apartment. He had only been gone a day, but he felt as if he had returned from a marathon. The fatigue was overwhelming. He sat down heavily in his old easy chair.

When he awoke, the sun was shining through a thin sliver where the curtains had not quite been drawn completely together. It was early morning. It took a moment for him to reorient himself and to remember how he had ended up in his own living room.

Then it dawned on Jack what he had to do.

First he called Valerie. She would want a full report of his adventures, he knew. She would be heading to work at this time of day, but they could plan to discuss all that had transpired over dinner. He had other things on his mind as well.

Valerie Cummins sounded to be in a good mood.

"Welcome back, partner. How are things in the Hollywood Hills?" she asked.

"Didn't see them," Jack replied. "Saw a lot of other

interesting things. Went some places I wouldn't want to visit again. You might get a kick out of them, though."

"Where on earth was that, Jack?"

"Tell ya when we get together. I hope we can do that this evening. I've been missing you," Jack said.

"Aw, that's so good to hear," Valerie said, sounding genuinely pleased. "It's been ages."

"It's been a little over thirty-six hours, to be exact," Jack said.

"Well, seems longer when you're not with me."

Jack could hear the smile in Valerie's voice. He hadn't enjoyed the separation either.

"Ordinarily I'd make you take me out for dinner. You did, after all, leave me to fend for myself," she said. "But, I'm going to be tired after this shift. And I bet you won't have got over your fatigue by tonight either. Bring me a pizza—all dressed. See you at half past six. Don't be late."

"It's a date," Jack said. "I've got a lot of stuff to discuss. I hope you're going to be in a listening mood."

"I'll try," she said. "Well, gotta go. Duty calls. I'll see you tonight. Love ya."

"Me too," Jack said. And she was gone.

He hung up and dialed the police station, hoping to catch Ted Brown before things got too hectic. Keegan Willis answered Jack's call.

"He had a late night," Willis said. "Spent a lot of time down in the cells with a friend of yours, from what I hear. He'll be in a little later. If you're heading this way, he might have arrived by the time you drag your sorry self in here. I figure you want to tell us all about your trip to the land of sun, surf, and movie stars."

"Try desert, windmills, and collection agencies, for a start," Jack said, regretting he had fallen into the detective's trap again. Willis enjoyed getting Jack's blood pressure to rise.

"Hate to be the bearer of bad news," Willis said. "Maybe I should make you wait for my boss, but what the heck. We haven't got the girl yet. Looks like you went on your little excursion for nothing. Fretz clammed up on us. Said he'd thought better of trusting Herties, you, or us to give him a fair deal. I don't know what he could be thinking. He says he won't talk—not yet at least. Says he wants to think about his next move."

"Seems to me, his next move will be to a more secure facility, if he keeps that up," Jack said. "Are you guys doing anything to try and find the girl?"

"No. We're just sitting back, eating doughnuts and drinking coffee all day. What do you think, Jack? Of course we're trying to track her down, but we've got no leads and so far we're coming up empty. What are you going to do?" Willis asked.

"That's an interesting question, coming from you. I have every intention of doing something about it, but before I go, I've got a question."

"Make it fast, Sherlock," Willis replied.

"I left this police department under a cloud of suspicion. Folks said I had been dealing drugs when I had that little run-in with Lorentini's baseball bat. I found myself on the street soon enough."

"Your point?" Willis asked.

"My point," Jack said, "is that Ted Brown has been bending the rules by letting me in on some of these cases lately, and you, for all your bluster and insinuation, have appeared rather flexible, yourself—like just now. What gives?"

"Let me level with you, Jack. I never really believed you were working with the bad guys. Ted certainly never did, and he told me so. I just had this one problem with you."

"What was that?" Jack asked, genuinely confused.

"You never fought. You just let it happen. You let them put you out. For a while I called you the shopping cart, because it seemed to me you just let people push you around. There, I've said it, and you'll never let me get away with being tough with you ever again."

"Well, Valerie was right, I guess. You're not so bad after all," Jack said. "Will you let me be thankful for your honesty? Thanks for being a friend—a better one than I imagined. Better than I guess I've been to you."

"Don't go all mushy on me, Elton. I don't want to have to hit you," Keegan Willis replied.

Jack could tell by now when the detective was trying to put on a show of bravado. Maybe it was a sign that things were going to get better.

I've been undercover, and not even I knew it, he thought.

"Gotta go rescue a damsel in distress," he said. "Is that okay with you, Officer?"

"Get off my phone," Willis said. And Jack knew the detective was smiling.

Chapter Twenty-four
Come Out, Come Out, Wherever You Are

Fretz wasn't talking—at all. He didn't want to be bothered, he said, when he was asked if he would like to have a visitor.

That visitor was Jack Elton, and Jack was determined that he was going to find Jennifer Herties with or without Bernard Fretz's help. It was now settled that it would be without.

He headed to the detective division to ask Willis for some details of the search so far.

"Just tell me where you've been looking. I'll at least know where she's not, assuming that you've looked in these places after Fretz was under your watchful eye in the cells."

"She's not in the box," Willis said, referring to the oversize casket affair that Jen had apparently been locked into when they had attempted to track the cell phone call Fretz had allowed her to make to her father. "We hauled that away after we found it."

"What else?" Jack asked.

"We're checking with all her friends. Showing them Fretz's picture to see if they've seen him before. We want to know if they've seen him since all this happened. We're looking for anyone who was acquainted with our new guest, as well. Folks from work. People he might have associated with. Anyone he might have let it slip to that he had a new fund-raising scheme."

"Any luck?" Jack asked.

"You see Jennifer Herties sitting around here? No, we haven't had any luck. It breaks my heart to say this, but maybe you will have better results. You always seem to find an angle we didn't think of," Willis said.

"You said she's not in the box. I wonder. A couple more questions and I'll be gone."

"Shoot," Willis replied.

"Did you impound his truck?"

"Absolutely. It's evidence."

"Find any tools?"

"Boatloads. The guy was a regular handyman," Willis said. "He musta been planning the abduction for a while, but he only decided on the box thing when the heat turned up. In spite of that, he put a lot of work into it. I saw it before it went to be taken apart by the evidence guys. I wish I could build stuff like that on the spur of the moment."

"I wonder where he buys his tools and supplies," Jack asked.

"Planning on taking up carpentry?"

"Nope. Got another idea. I may need some help from the department."

"We'll see," Willis said. "Depends on what kind of help."

"I'll let you know. Gotta go," Jack replied.

Before he headed out toward what had been, until recently, Fretz's neighborhood, Jack made a trip to the impound lot of the police department and spoke to the attendant in charge.

Todd MacMillan was a large man in overalls. A former cop who had been sidelined by a stray bullet that had left him with a limp and a pension, Todd had refused to let his misfortune keep him from being involved in the profession he loved, even if it was only as an onlooker.

He was in charge of the vehicles that were collected by the department as they attempted to solve crime or investigate motor vehicle accidents. He loved to hear the stories the officers told about the cars and trucks they had had towed into the big lot.

"It helps ma feel like I'm still part o' the force—those tales the laddies tell," he had once told Jack in his thick Scottish brogue.

"Todd, me laddie, could I have a look at that pickup over there for a moment?" Jack asked as the two men stood by the big steel gate at the front of the lot and squinted into the sun.

"I suppose you may," Todd replied. "Just don't go messin' around with anything. The evidence guys have done their fingerprinting and filled their little zippered baggies with stuff that might be important, but I'd feel better if you wore these on your mitts, if you need to look at anything."

He walked over and pulled a pair of blue latex gloves from a box sitting on the sill of the tiny cubicle that served only to keep him out of the noonday heat and keep the endless reams of forms that had to be filled in order to keep track of all that was stored within the impound lot.

Jack pulled on the gloves and headed for the truck. He climbed into the back and began carefully examining some of Fretz's tools. He gingerly opened boxes and peered inside, sometimes picking out an implement, reading the manufacturer's mark, and gently replacing it in its original location.

A few moments later, he jumped down from the truck and walked over to his friend, who had been watching from the main gate, occasionally lifting his old, stained baseball cap and mopping his almost totally bald head.

"I've got what I need, Todd. Thanks a bunch. I'll buy you a haggis for Robbie Burns Day."

"Don't bother," the man said. "I've got better things than another stomach to put in my own stomach. Promise me a steak. If you're going to promise something that you're not going to deliver, I'd rather it be a steak."

"Consider it done," Jack said, thrusting out his hand and grinning broadly.

Todd MacMillan took the hand with a grip like a vise and shook it violently before letting Jack go free.

Jack walked out of the lot, massaging his hand, and headed for his car.

Jack knew there was only a small chance that his hunch would lead anywhere, but with the pressure of time and Fretz's reticence about revealing the location of his captive, he felt it was better to be doing something other than sitting. No one knew when, or even if, the kidnapper would break his silence.

What can he be thinking? Jack wondered as he drove toward one of the larger shopping malls on the outskirts of the city. *Surely he doesn't think he's improving his chances of striking a bargain.*

Jack parked his car in the massive lot surrounding the shopping center and headed for the major hardware store that was one of the mall's anchor tenants. The business's presence was proclaimed by a bright orange-and-white sign. The trademark sign was familiar to anyone who had ever considered home renovation, and the company's sponsorship of NASCAR racing and community causes like Habitat for Humanity made it recognizable to others.

Jack headed for the CUSTOMER SERVICE sign that hung near the check-out desks by the main entrance.

A young man wearing an orange apron with the name Gavin written in permanent marker on the front inquired how he might be of assistance.

"I don't know if you can help, but let's give it a try," Jack said.

"I'll do my best, sir. As you can see, we have just about anything you might need for your construction and renovation needs. We pride ourselves on service, and if we don't have what you're . . ."

"I'm not buying today," Jack said.

The young man's face fell.

"I need some information, if you have it," Jack continued. "It's police business."

Gavin looked interested. "How can I help?" he asked.

"Have you heard of a man named Fretz? Bernard Fretz. He apparently does a lot of wood working. Buys high-end, quality stuff. The sort of thing you folks deal in."

"That would be hard to say," Gavin replied. "This is a big place. We get a lot of customers in here. It's not like your old country store where everyone knows everybody else."

"Do you think someone in your carpentry or power tools section might be able to help?" Jack asked.

"Let's give it a try," Gavin said with a smile. He headed down one of the long aisles.

Jack trailed behind, marvelling at the variety of materials available to those who made things for a living or a hobby.

Gavin drew up next to a short, beachball-shaped man with a bushy mustache and a bald head fringed with curly black hair. His apron proclaimed TONY in a stylized felt marker script.

Tony was talking animatedly to an older man. The conversation appeared to center on the relative merits of two brands of routers. Tony had a favorite. The customer was looking for something less expensive.

Gavin waited for a lull in the conversation before approaching his co-worker and speaking conspiratorially in his ear.

Tony looked over at Jack and gave a little nod before returning to his lecture about torque, depth adjustments, and lifetime warranties.

Gavin smiled at Jack and returned to his post by the check-outs.

Eventually, it appeared that the sales associate had closed the deal on a new router. The customer moved on to the cash, apparently satisfied that he had been well served.

"How can I be of assistance?" Tony asked.

Jack explained that he was trying to determine whether Fretz had been a customer here. He was especially interested to know if the man had made any purchases recently.

"Gee, buddy, I see a lot of folks in here in a week. You expect me to remember one guy who might have bought a file or some sandpaper or even a nice router like this one?"

He hefted the electric tool in his hand. He had not had the chance to replace it on the shelf after his precious customer.

"I'm not sure what I expected," Jack said. "I was sort of hoping that he might be a regular customer and that perhaps someone might remember him."

"Sorry, bud. The name don't mean much to me. Sure I can't sell you something?"

"Thanks," Jack said and turned to go.

"You might check with Gavin," Tony called after him. "Maybe the guy's got an account here."

Jack headed for the customer service desk again.

"I probably shouldn't be doing this," Gavin said over the top of the monitor. "I can check the name and let you know if it's here. Not much else I can give you without some kind of warrant, you understand."

"Anything would be a help," Jack said.

"Well, you won't need a court order, I guess. I'll tell you everything I know."

"That's great," Jack said too quickly.

"There's nothing here. No Bernard Fretz in the computer. If you need an address, I can lend you a phone book, though."

"That won't be necessary. I was just hoping . . ."

Gavin continued. "Now, ordinarily I wouldn't suggest this. But seeing as you're not buying anyway, I might suggest you go to . . ."

At this point, the young man lowered his voice, looked around to see if anyone was watching, and whispered the name of a competitor to Jack.

"I know where they are," Jack said. "Thanks for the help."

"Think of us the next time you're doing any renovations," Gavin said, before turning to help a man wearing bib overalls and a baseball cap that looked as if they had both been laundered in house paint and grease.

Jack made his way across town to the warehouse-size edifice of yet another hardware retailer.

Why didn't I come here first? Jack thought as he pulled into the parking lot. *It's closer to Fretz's house. It would be more logical for him to do business here.*

Jack was greeted by the same type of environment he had encountered at the previous location. Shelves and racks spanned ceiling to floor. The sales associates wore shop aprons. It smelled of wood, glue, and paint. The color scheme was blue and white this time.

Her name was Melinda and she asked how she might help. Jack noticed that the names were printed on plastic badges here.

"I'm looking for some information," he said.

Melinda's expression did not change. She said she would do what she could.

Jack went through the talk he had rehearsed at the previous location.

"Let me take you back to Randy," she said. "He knows everybody. If anyone can help, Randy can."

She escorted Jack between the rows to the power tool section and introduced him to a young man who looked like he lifted trucks for exercise. To say he was muscular would be an understatement. He had the reddest hair Jack had ever seen.

"He's a football player," Melinda said, smiling up at Randy with admiration in her eyes. Then she turned and left the two men to talk.

Jack introduced himself.

"I'm looking for information about someone who might have been one of your customers. It's really important."

"I'll do what I can. Who are you looking for?" Randy asked.

"This guy's a cabinetmaker of sorts. It's a hobby, I think. I've only heard about his work. Apparently, he's good."

Jack told Randy the area of town where Fretz had been living. The young man nodded his recognition of the area.

"His name is Bernard Fretz. Ring any bells?"

The young man's eyes went wide.

"You don't mean Bernie? He's got that house over on the side of the mountain. Oh, yeah. I know Bernie. Didn't know his last name till just now, though."

"I guess that's the guy," Jack said. "Think can help?"

Randy was still going on enthusiastically.

"Good old Bernie. Haven't seen him for a day or two."

"A day or two? He was that regular?" Jack asked.

"Oh, yeah. He always had some project on the go. Said it kept his mind occupied. Poor guy. Used to work for some bigwig in the city. Then he got fired. Couldn't get another job to save his soul. At least that's what he told me."

"You say he was here a couple of days ago?"

"Something like that. Time flies when you're having fun. Coulda been a little longer."

"What sort of stuff does he buy?" Jack asked.

"Well, he did a lot of woodworking. Bought a lot of lumber. Good stuff. He always went for the high end when it came to tools. Lately it's been stuff to renovate his place. I hear he's planning on moving."

"Do you remember what he bought the last time he was here?"

"That's easy," Randy said. "Locks."

"Locks," Jack said for confirmation. "So he was changing the locks before he moved."

"Maybe, but I doubt it," the clerk replied.

"Why?"

"Wrong kind of locks."

"Padlocks?" Jack asked, envisioning Jen Herties in another of Fretz's works of cabinetry.

"Nope. Door locks. But not what you'd want on your front door."

"Why is that?" Jack asked, hoping to get to Randy's punch line before the store closed for the day.

"He bought double cylinder deadbolts. I mean locks that use a key on both sides. You know how a door might have a lock on the outside to throw the deadbolt and a knob on the inside so you can get out? Well Bernie bought locks that use the key on both sides. Here. Let me show you."

Randy led Jack down an aisle lined with door fittings until they came to a display with a number of miniature doors set into small frames.

He patted the top of one of the displays.

"This here's a Weiser Model 4371. As you can see, it opens with this key." Randy turned the key to demonstrate. He opened the little door to reveal that the opposite side looked exactly the same.

"Over here is our Model 4471. It's a single cylinder. There is a keyhole on one side and a knob on the other." He repeated his demonstration for Jack's benefit.

"Why would you want one of those?" Jack asked.

"Well, you probably wouldn't use it for a front door. Too much of a hassle to get a key every time you want to open the door. No, you'd put this on a side or back door where there might be a window close. If a bad guy comes along, wanting to break in, he busts the window and reaches around to throw the deadbolt. You put in a double cylinder lock and he's got nothing to turn. Of course, you've got to make sure you take the key out of the lock or you defeat the purpose."

"So, once these things are locked, you need a key to get either in or out," Jack said.

"That's about it," Randy said. "They build these things tough. Unless you've got a good hacksaw and lots of time, you're pretty much stuck."

"Did Bernie buy anything else when he was here?"

"Nothing stands out at the moment. It was the locks

that intrigued me. I sort of wondered about that. But when he explained it to me, it all made sense. Smart guy, that Bernie."

"He had an explanation for buying the double cylinder deadbolts?" Jack asked.

"Yeah. Wanted to make sure no one got in while he was gone. Figured that having to use a key on both sides would be less of a hassle than cleaning up after an intruder."

"But he's planning on selling his place. The new owners can deal with all that, don't you think?"

"Oh, he's not selling that place. He needs somewhere to stay until he finds a home in town," Randy replied.

"I'm confused," Jack said. "Are we talking about the same place—up on the mountain? He said he was selling it."

"Oh, that place. Yeah. He mentioned that he had a prospective buyer. No. I meant his other place."

"What other place?" Jack could feel the heat rising above his collar. His heart had suddenly begun to beat a lot faster.

"Don't you know? He's got that cottage of his, by the lake, a couple of hours north. I've never seen it, but he always liked to talk about how he . . ."

"Thanks. Gotta go," Jack said, fleeing from the store and a dazed-looking Randy.

"Get me Brown or Willis. Now!" Jack fairly yelled into his cell phone once he had reached his car. "If they're not there, page them. If they can't be paged, get me whoever is in command. It's urgent."

Jack started the vehicle and headed out toward the main highway. He turned north, unaware of exactly where his final destination was. He held the phone to his ear with one hand and steered with the other.

"Brown here," came the voice over the receiver.

"Not much time, Ted. You gotta get me some information and then follow me on the double."

"Hang on there, Hopalong. What's this all about?"

"Fretz has another place, north of the city. You've gotta get me an address. Call me back when you've got it. Then I need you to check in Fretz's personal effects for keys. New ones. Make sure they are tagged as evidence. Bring any keys you find when you come."

"Okay. Okay." Brown's voice told Jack that the detective was catching on to what the private investigator seemed to be suggesting. "I've passed a note just now to one of the officers. They'll check land registry. Just pray Fretz used his own name. I'll look for keys and start after you. Don't break any laws."

"I don't know where I'm going, so I won't dare speed—yet," Jack replied.

"Don't speed at all. You know how that could get you slowed down real quick."

"No promises. I've got friends in high places. You are in a high place, aren't you, Ted?"

"I'll call you as soon as I get your directions. If you hear sirens, it might be me. If it's not, you're on your own."

The line went dead.

Chapter Twenty-five
I Love It When a Plan Comes Together

Jack drove north, trying to be careful not to press too hard on the accelerator. He felt tense all over. Fretz had stonewalled and was placing Jennifer Herties in greater danger with each passing moment. Now that he felt close to the resolution of the problem, he was traveling on a mystery tour, unsure of where to turn—unsure whether he had traveled too far.

Time was passing, and he was getting nervous about the fact that his phone had not rung since he had spoken to Ted Brown.

"Come on. Find the address. Let's go, guys," Jack spoke to himself as he drove from the outskirts of the city, through the suburbs to the north, and into the long stretch of highway that led to cottage country. Traffic thinned. He tapped nervously on the steering wheel, willing the cell phone to ring.

When it did, he startled and felt his heart trip into high gear.

"I hope it's good news," he said, not bothering to confirm that it was the call he had been waiting for.

"It's news," Ted Brown's voice said. "Whether it's good or not, only time will tell. Got an address for you. Think you can remember it, or should I wait for you to pull over so you can write?"

"I'm good," Jack said, taking his hand off the wheel and digging for a pen in his shirt pocket. He set the phone on the passenger seat, grabbed the wheel with his left hand, and leaned over to open the glove compartment. After some digging, he found a piece of paper.

"Go ahead," he said into the receiver once he had all his gear together.

"I just did. Weren't you listening?" Brown asked.

"Sorry, I got distracted. Traffic, you know."

He pressed the speaker button on the phone and laid it on the passenger seat. Steering with his left hand, he managed to write the directions echoing from the wireless apparatus on the scrap of paper he balanced on his leg, alternating his gaze between the windshield and the note.

"I'll meet you there," Brown said. "I got tied up at the office before I left. Wait till I get there."

"I know the area," Jack said and punched the END button on the phone. Then he pressed his foot to the floor.

Fretz's cottage was well off the main road. While the route was well maintained, it was paved with gravel.

Jack was impatient to be at the house, but the flying stones kept up a din that was almost unbearable, and he had to slow down. He wound his way up the side of a mountain overlooking a small lake.

Guy's got good taste in real estate, he thought. *Too bad he won't get to come back here for the foreseeable future, if ever.*

The cottage sat on a small plot of land in the midst of an area surrounded by pine trees. It appeared to be a single-story log house. There was a covered porch before the front door. As Jack walked up the pine-needle-strewn path, he could see the bright brass lock that Fretz had installed. On closer examination, Jack could see that it was a duplicate of the one Randy had shown him a little earlier. He had to walk around to the right side of the building and look through the small window to see that it did indeed have a matching keyhole on its inner surface.

But that was all he could verify. There was no sign of Jennifer Herties, at least not from the vantage point of what appeared to be one of only two windows in the entire structure. A mate for the one he was peering through was visible across what appeared to be a combination kitchen and sitting room.

Brown still had not arrived. Jack decided to explore. He continued around the building. There were no more windows. Even though it was apparent that there were rooms in the back of the house, it seemed as if Fretz had neglected to make any provision for natural light. Perhaps it was simply because of the dense forest behind the cabin, Jack reasoned.

It couldn't be possible that he was planning this all along, he thought.

Jack tried to knock on the back wall. He only succeeded

in knocking some bark off the rough log and grazing his knuckles. The wood was solid. The only sound was of flesh meeting log. If the girl was inside, this would not be the way to communicate. The spaces between the logs had been caulked with some sort of cement, to complicate things even more.

The building had been supplied with electricity. A single wire snaked in through a conduit at the peak of the roof. An outhouse stood, door ajar, at the end of a path, further back in the trees.

As Jack came around the corner of the cabin, he could hear the sound of a high-powered engine. It wasn't a truck. He was sure of that. And it was making good time coming up the incline. It could only be Detective Ted Brown in his department car, he thought.

A few moments later, the white Crown Victoria rounded the last turn in the path to Fretz's cabin. The tires spun. It leapt over a tree root, bottomed out with a loud bang, and came to rest just behind Jack's own vehicle.

Brown unfolded himself from behind the wheel and walked toward the private investigator standing by the front entrance, as if this was Friday night and the boys were gathering for a weekend of fishing.

The passenger door of the police car swung open, and a female officer stepped out onto the path.

"Hi, Jack," the detective said. "I see you made it here in good time. This is Constable Douglas. That's her last name, before you make any smart remarks. She's here to help, in case we need a female officer."

Jack smiled at the officer and nodded.

"Anything to report, Jack?"

"Not much," he replied. "The girl is not readily visible from the outside. That is, if she is even in there. I notice there are two closed doors at the back of the room." He motioned toward one of the side windows and Brown followed him.

As the detective peered into the house, Jack continued. "As you can see, there is one door with a regular passage set, a doorknob and no sign of a lock. That other one, on the right, is outfitted like the front door. It has a double cylinder deadbolt, I think. That means it needs a key, no matter which side you're on. Handy if you want to keep someone on the other side and be relatively certain they stay there."

"Okay, Jack, we're going in," the detective said. "I took some extra precautions before I left. That's why I'm a little late. I have a search warrant. I have a bunch of keys. And I made sure we have enough copies of Fretz's signature on his booking slip to be sure he can't deny they belong to him. Any idea which key is which?"

He reached into a brown padded envelope he was carrying and pulled out a sealed evidence bag with two key rings in it.

"Officer Douglas," Brown called to the young woman, "I want you to witness the opening of this bag, in case there are any questions later. I've got some papers for you to sign."

The three huddled by the door as the detective opened a pocketknife and slit the red tape sealing the envelope. He looked at his watch and noted the time, which he wrote on a sheet of paper he had extracted from the envelope. He then presented the document for the officer to sign before putting his name on it too.

"The key will have a square head on it, and will have the name Weiser in block letters. It will be fairly shiny. It's new," Jack suggested.

"I got four like that," Brown said. "Guess we just try the process of elimination."

"You're probably looking at two sets of two keys," Jack said.

The detective approached the door and inserted a key. It went all the way in but would not turn the tumbler.

"One down. Three to go," Brown said.

Jack held up both hands with fingers crossed.

Ted Brown inserted the key in the lock and gave it a twist. The deadbolt slid out of the latch with a solid *click*. He pushed on the door, and it squeaked open.

Inside the building, everything looked to be in order. Fretz liked to keep a neat house, or so it appeared.

A large table stood in the middle of the floor. Four sturdy wooden chairs were placed around it. A metal basin sat on the sideboard, for dishwashing, Jack assumed. Wooden cupboards hung over the counter to the right.

Two easy chairs sat on a small carpet facing a stone fireplace on the left wall. A rather moth-eaten deer head hung over the mantle.

"Hello," Brown called out. "Anybody here?"

There was no answer, but Jack thought he heard a sound, like a board creaking or a small creature crying. He went to the door with the lock on it.

First he pushed on it. It was unyielding.

Then he hammered on it with his fist. This time, he was

sure he heard a noise. It was weak, but he definitely heard something.

"The keys," he called to Brown. "Where are the keys?"

The detective moved to the door and inserted one of the square-headed keys into the lock.

He was successful on the first try. The door swung open. All three stared into the small room that lay beyond.

The sound came again—louder now. Its source was a small bundle curled up on the bare floor. She was blindfolded and her mouth was taped closed, but otherwise she was unencumbered.

Jack ran into the room and removed the blindfold. The girl's eyes flew open and she stared in fear, or surprise. Jack couldn't be sure which.

He eased the tape from her mouth as best he could, but it caught and the girl winced and gave another little cry.

"Jennifer? Jennifer Herties?" It was Brown who was asking.

She nodded and uttered a whispered, "Yes."

"We're here to take you home," Jack said.

Tears rolled down Jennifer Herties' cheeks, and she nodded her understanding.

Brown turned her over into the care of Officer Douglas, who led the unsteady girl out to the back of the cabin.

Jack and Ted Brown stayed behind to wait for the two women's return.

The detective called into the city for a team to secure the site and collect evidence.

"I'll stay behind and wait for the others to arrive, Jack. Douglas will take the girl in the squad car. You head back too. You don't need to hang around."

"Who gets to tell Herties his girl is safe?" Jack asked.

"Tell you what. You give him a call once you get down the mountain. If he's in his office, go and stay with him. Let him know he's to expect a call from us momentarily. If he's at home, I guess you can give him the same message, but don't go dropping by without an invitation."

"That will be easy," Jack said. "I'm not sure where he lives."

Jennifer and the female officer returned from their short trip and headed for the police car. The constable opened the passenger door so the girl could get in and then produced a package of wet wipes from the glove compartment and handed one to her.

Jennifer smiled weakly as she struggled to put on her seat belt.

The officer got a nod from Brown, indicating that she could leave, and backed the Ford to where she could turn around. She headed down the slope, speaking into her microphone all the way.

"Guess it's my turn now," Jack said.

"Thanks, Jack. You did good," Brown said, holding out his hand.

"You're welcome, Ted. Glad I could be of assistance. I'll let you guys do the media thing. Just put in a good word with Herties when you see him, okay?"

"Sure. Now go home, or wherever it is you're headed. And drive carefully. You don't want to ruin the celebration."

Jack walked to his car and negotiated his way down the hill. The sun was beginning to settle just above the western horizon as he turned onto the highway and headed south.

Chapter Twenty-six
I Feel So Broke up, I Wanna Go Home

As it turned out, Wolf Herties was still in his office when Jack's call was put through. The man sounded distraught and tired from the stress he had been under for so long.

"I hope you've got some encouraging news, Jack. I need something to give me hope at this point."

Jack could hardly contain himself.

"I've got more than hope for you, sir. I've got your daughter."

"You do? That's wonderful, miraculous, tremendous. Oh, dear, I don't know what to say or do. I'm. I'm just so happy!"

"Well, actually I don't have her with me. She's with the police right now. I suspect she'll go through a debriefing this evening. She'll likely spend an evening under observation in the hospital, and then if everything is all right you'll get to take her home."

253

"Can I see her?"

"That's not up to me, obviously. I've been told to advise you that the police will be in touch shortly. They'll probably wait until Jennifer has had a preliminary check-up so they can answer some of your questions. I'll be downtown shortly. I'd like to come up to see you."

"My good man, that is something you are welcome to do anytime. I'll be waiting for you. Let's have dinner and celebrate. I'll order in to the boardroom.

The evening was a time of celebration. Wolf Herties was happier than Jack had ever seen him. He sat and reminisced about Jennifer's growing up, about her successes and even some of her failures.

The police had called and gave the staff doctor's assessment that, apart from dehydration, hunger, and exhaustion, Jennifer was in remarkably good shape. They suggested that he wait until the next day to see her. She would need the night to rest. In fact, she had fallen asleep the moment they had taken her to her private room in the hospital. They assured the anxious father that when he saw his daughter, he would be able to take her home.

The two men talked a little longer, and Jack suggested that they should both get some sleep before the exciting day ahead.

"Thank you, Jack," the millionaire said as the two of them parted company. "I appreciate everything you have done. And I can't forget how much help Eric has been. If he hadn't cared enough to pursue this, who knows how it might have turned out. Please let him know how much I appreciate what he did too."

"I will, sir," Jack said. "And, who knows? Maybe you'll have the opportunity to thank him in person."

"I'd like to do that. I really would. Maybe you can work something out between the two of you, and we can get together for dinner again. Next time it will be in better surroundings than the boardroom, though."

The two men parted company and agreed to meet at the police station the next morning.

The following day, it was some time before Herties and Jack could get in to the detective division to talk to Ted Brown and Keegan Willis, let alone see Jennifer.

The task of taking statements and filling in endless forms, though tedious and time-consuming, was nevertheless necessary. And the officers were being extremely careful to be sure they got it all right before they could take time for pleasantries.

Willis despised the paperwork more than any. His favorite instruction, to those who were called upon to fill in police forms, was, "Press hard. You're making three hundred copies." His attempts at humor got tiresome for his co-workers, but Willis always found his own jokes a cause for laughter.

Mercifully, it was Detective Sergeant Brown who was called upon to administer the paperwork that Wolf Herties had to fill in before he could get his daughter back.

"You will need to keep yourself available for further

interviews and, of course, for the trial," Brown said. "I think you'll find that your daughter will appreciate your support in dealing with the trauma she has suffered and with the questioning she will unfortunately need to undergo from us, and the lawyers, as time goes by."

"I'll make sure that I'm available for whatever you might require, Sergeant. And, you can be sure that Jen's mother and I will give her all the support we can. Now, when can I see my daughter?"

"Just a few more things we need to finish up first," Brown replied.

The time seemed to drag for Jack. He had been through all this so many times before, from the other side of the desk.

Though he had never had to deal with a kidnapping, he had seen his fair share of robberies; a few murders, including that nasty business involving his friend Brendan Biggs; and more traffic-related crimes than he cared to think about.

It was later that afternoon before Jennifer and her father were reunited.

When a female officer ushered Jen into the waiting area, the girl threw herself into her father's arms and hugged him tightly, tears welling up in her dark eyes.

It was some time before either one loosened their grip on the other. Their voices were muffled from their faces being buried in each other's shoulders.

Jack could only stand and watch the happy reunion.

Eventually, wiping his eyes with a handkerchief that he had produced from a back pocket, Wolf Herties turned toward Jack and said, "Jack Elton, I'd like you to meet my daughter."

"Pleased to meet you," Jack said and stood, looking at a loss for what to do next as the young woman reestablished her hold on her father.

When she finally let the man loose from the embrace, Jennifer Herties turned toward Jack.

"Thank you," she said and gripped Jack's outstretched hand in both of hers. "They tell me you had a lot to do with getting me away from that man."

It was clear that part of the time spent in the police station had been used to try to remove some of the more visible signs of her imprisonment.

Jen had obviously had the opportunity to shower and wash her hair, which was now tied back in a ponytail.

One of the female officers had found a pair of sweatpants for her. She was also wearing a blue T-shirt, with the name and crest of the police department stenciled on the front.

Everyone laughed as Jen turned around to show the back of the shirt. Written there in bold white lettering were the words *BOMB SQUAD. If you see me running, try to keep up.*

The tension of the day's events, and those that had led up to the girl's return, had begun to ease.

Jennifer Herties was duly signed over into the care of her father.

Wolf Herties thanked the police officers, and together Jack, the father, and the daughter headed out into the afternoon sun.

Jen promised to let her dad do all the talking when her mother returned from Europe.

"I'll be in touch," Herties said when the car pulled up in front of the tower bearing his name. "I want to assure you that I am extremely thankful for what you've done for me and Jennifer."

"I'll be waiting for your call," Jack said. "But, if I might make a suggestion, sir. Take your daughter home. Help her deal with the trauma of the past few days. We have time. You have time. Spend it with Jennifer."

"Thanks, Jack," was Herties' only reply.

"Thanks, sir," Jennifer said and patted Jack's shoulder before sliding out of the backseat and walking, hand-in-hand with her father, into the golden glass tower.

Jack knew he would have to call in his favor soon, but not today.

Chapter Twenty-seven
All Dressed—and Nowhere to Go

"*Of all the good things that have happened today, I'm going to enjoy this most.*"

Jack hummed along with the car radio as he drove east to the apartment block where Valerie lived.

He had learned, from sad experience, not to take any chances when it came to her favorite fast food. He had made some dreadful choices in the past and had been fortunate that none of the really bad pizzas had ended up on her plate.

There was a little place owned by a nice Italian family just a few blocks from Valerie's apartment. They had discovered it together one night as they walked through the neighborhood after a busy day. Valerie had wanted neither to cook nor to stay home for supper. They went out in search of sustenance.

And there it had been, on the corner of the block. It had looked good through the window. The aromas wafting onto the sidewalk had been tantalizing. Jack had decided it was worth taking a chance and suggested that this be their dining place for the evening.

They had fallen in love with the food. They declared it "our pizza place" and became regular customers, getting to know the owner and his wife in the process.

It was to Ristorante Colombini that Jack was headed now. His instructions had been clear. "Bring me a pizza. All dressed," she had said. So that is what he told Maria Colombini when she had answered his call a while earlier.

"Make it special. It's for my girl, and I've just come back from a trip away," he had said.

"Oh, Giovanni," Maria had replied. "You should marry that girl. I see her always making the eyes at you. She's in love. I think you in love too, maybe, eh?"

"But I love your pizza. Run away with me," Jack had teased.

"Believe me, Giovanni." She always called him by the Italian version of his name. "Franco Colombini is enough of a handful to deal with. You marry that police lady. Have little police babies. You need to settle down. Your parcel will be ready when you arrive. See you then."

Almost twenty minutes later, Jack pulled up to the eatery and went inside. He was given a large square box and a short lecture from Maria about not wasting time getting it to its final destination. He paid and fled down the street.

When Jack arrived on Valerie's floor, she was waiting for him outside her apartment door. They hugged awkwardly while he tried not to drop their dinner.

Valerie had set the table with silverware and candles. A

small bottle of wine stood on the counter awaiting Jack's ministrations with the corkscrew.

When he finally set down the box and slipped out of his coat, Valerie gave him a proper welcome hug. He did not resist. Maria Colombini's words sat below the surface of Jack's consciousness.

"I'm under orders to eat this while it's hot," he said.

"How romantic," Valerie replied.

"It's just that Maria said we should . . ."

"I'm teasing, silly. Besides, I'm famished. Eat first. Talk later. Did she call you Giovanni?"

Jack smiled.

The meal was soon over. They had not talked much. Apart from comparing the difference in temperatures between Vancouver and Los Angeles and some general comments about his trip, Jack had not offered any details of what he had discovered.

For her part, Valerie had had a couple of rather routine days in his absence. She had missed lunch and used that as her excuse for eating so quickly and saying so little.

Once the coffee had been brewed, the couple retired to the couch, where they sat close. Jack put his arm around Valerie. She put her head on his shoulder.

"Want to hear about my trip?" he asked.

"Not really," she replied. "I've got a general idea of what happened. I heard that Schreiver was experiencing a little bit of payback for his transgressions. I know that Jen Herties is back home with Daddy. I'd love to hear how he explains all of this to his wife."

"Shall we choose another topic of conversation, or do you want to continue talking shop?" Jack asked.

"Sure, I want to know about that 'make it all up to you' stuff you were using on me before you left on your California adventure."

"Oh, that," he said. "I've been meaning to talk to you about something that's been on my mind—a sort of plan. I think it might make it up to you. I've got to make some more arrangements. Herties owes me a favor. I'm thinking he can help out."

"A tour of his vault? A ride in his car? Where does he fit into our relationship?" she asked.

"You are kidding. Right?" Jack felt a lump in the pit of his stomach.

"Sort of, Jack. But I think you need to come to the point. I'm beginning to feel like I'm playing second fiddle to a lot of other folks. I have my job and you have yours. And I can accept that. What I want to know is, do you see our relationship continuing and growing? If you do, and if you want me to care about you, my first suggestion would be to slow down a little, before my poor, dear Jack makes himself sick."

She smiled now, but her genuine concern had been impressed on Jack's consciousness.

There were things Jack had wanted to say. There were plans he had wanted to share, feelings he had been unable to express.

The next few days found him feeling sorry for himself when he should have been elated over the happy resolution of the kidnapping of Jennifer Herties.

He tried to convince himself that it was the sudden drop in adrenaline that accounted for his state of mind.

But Jack knew there was something else that had to be resolved before he would feel good again.

"You'll never believe what happened."

Jack had settled into the couch where he and Valerie had had to conclude their last conversation so quickly, a few days earlier.

"Try me," Valerie said, setting a tray of coffee and store-bought cookies on the table. "I'm sorry I didn't have time to bake."

"Wolf Herties and I had a little conversation a day or so ago," Jack said. "He told me that Ben Schreiver is coming back to this country."

"Doesn't sound good," Valerie said as she sat down beside Jack and took his hand in hers.

"That's the incredible part," Jack said. "I don't know all the details. But it seems like somehow there was an arrangement made to extradite Schreiver back here, to stand trial for the theft of Herties' money. I'm not sure how all that will work out. I am certain, though, that W. D. will have his lawyers working on an airtight case."

"Wow! I bet he's sorry he talked to you now. Schreiver, I mean. Herties will want you to testify, I suppose."

"Yeah. I think you've got that right. But I think I owe him that much," Jack replied, smiling down at the young woman whose head was leaned on his shoulder.

"You look happy. But shouldn't he owe you?" Valerie asked.

"Oh, yeah. I almost forgot. Mr. Herties was very thankful for the work I put in. I actually have a bank balance now."

"Did he tell you how to invest your newfound wealth?"

"No, but I've come to a decision. I'm thinking of entering into a new partnership. Your opinion is very important."

Valerie looked shocked.

"I thought you liked to work alone, Jack. I don't think bringing in a partner is very wise at this stage. Jack, you need to get your priorities straight," she said.

"Oh, I've got them pretty straight. I think my new partner will agree," Jack said.

"And just who, pray tell, is this partner you're getting into business with?" Val asked.

"Maybe I should explain," he replied.

"Please do," Valerie said. "I can't believe you are acting so foolishly."

"Love has a way of doing that," he said.

Valerie's mouth fell open at his words. It was clear that she still did not understand the man sitting beside her.

"Okay. I guess I've spent enough time beating around the bush. I hope you'll forgive me," he said.

"We'll see."

"Maybe this'll help," he said.

Jack fumbled to retrieve something from his shirt pocket.

He retrieved a small blue velvet-covered box and opened it so Valerie couldn't see.

"What have you done now, Jack? You know I can't wear jewelry to work. And we don't go out to enough fancy places that I would need something to impress other people with."

Jack slowly turned the box toward Valerie.

When she saw what Jack had in his hand, she stared in disbelief.

"This is for my new partner. That is, if you'll have me," Jack said as he slid the ring onto Valerie's finger. "Please say yes," he said, biting his lip and hoping.

Valerie smiled and hugged him tightly.